A NEW PAGE

AIMEE MACRAE

 Serenade Publishing

Serenade Publishing

www.serenadepublishing.com

MORE FROM SERENADE PUBLISHING

Brigadier Station Series

By Sarah Williams:

The Brothers of Brigadier Station

The Sky over Brigadier Station

The Legacies of Brigadier Station

Christmas at Brigadier Station (An Outback Christmas Novella)

The Outback Governess (A Sweet Outback Novella)

Heart of the Hinterland Series

By Sarah Williams:

The Dairy Farmer's Daughter

Their Perfect Blend

Beyond the Barre

A Dying Second Sun

by Peter A. Dowse

Winner Winner Chicken Dinner

by Sarah Jackson

A New Page

by Aimee MacRae

Middle Women

By Jack Garrety

Mim and Wiggy's Grand Adventure

By Jay McKenzie

For more information visit:

www.serenadepublishing.com

For my Love, thank you for being you.
And for all the dreamers out there... keep going.

CHAPTER 1

"Hey Mitch?"

"Yo!"

Poppy winced as the usual mouthful of scotch-finger biscuits Mitch had for breakfast dusted over a delivery of new fiction.

"What's this?" she asked, flicking the white envelope covering her keyboard into the air. It looked official.

"Dunno. Came in this morning's transit. How'd ya meeting with boss-man go?"

"Good, I guess. He wants us to take out more of the older looking books—make room for face-out displays and that sort of thing. He's happy that our foot-traffic stats are high. Lots of visitors and our memberships are increasing. I tried to argue that's because we currently have a good balance between books, free space and programs but it won't be long before we have more eBooks than physical books."

"I don't think the oldies around here will go for that."

"Well, go for it or not, this new guy has a defined vision for the future and we need to support it." Poppy shoved the envelope into her bag. She'd open it later.

She watched Mitch huff and snap another Scotch-Finger. "How'd it go when ya mentioned your big idea?"

Not wanting her junior to see how resigned she really felt, Poppy turned away. "The garden? Basically got laughed at."

The learning garden was a great idea and Poppy knew it. A library should be the hub of the community, and a garden would create opportunities for people to come together and learn new skills. The new director had thought it a waste of resources, adamant that the idea didn't align with their priorities for a city library.

"Anyway, Mitch. Time to put breakfast away." Poppy sighed and waited for Mitch to finish brushing the crumbs from his shirt. "We've got a lot to do setting up the new tech lab and 3D printer. This place needs to look like a digital showroom before the Mayor visits tomorrow."

"And what boss-man wants boss-man gets right?"

"Yep." Poppy offered a half-smile. "Come on. Might as well get started."

The next few hours were spent by Poppy pushing around tech equipment, relocating books, hiding exposed electrical cabling and stopping every five minutes to help customers with anything from their book reservations to passport applications and everything in between including helping people use their mobile phone and talking to those customers who visited the library just for conversation.

It was physically demanding shifting the big shelving units and Poppy cursed the people who had decided it was a good idea. None-the-less, they'd been given a directive to make room for the new flashy printing hub and Poppy wasn't about to argue the point after her disappointing meeting that morning. *At least this gives me a reason to avoid finishing the staff rosters for a bit.*

It was nearly two o'clock before Poppy sat down for lunch in front of her computer screen. She scrolled through a catalogue of the latest new non-fiction as forkfuls of supermarket salad made their way into her mouth.

"Loo-kah...leek-ah...li-ck-ahh...li...li-ck-ahh," she muttered to herself, trying to perfect the pronunciation of the Danish word for happiness, lykke, and title of the book that had flashed up on her screen.

I'd love some Danish Lykke in my life, sighed Poppy as images of candlelit suppers; mugs of cocoa and baskets of homegrown vegetables came to her mind.

She wondered if fairy lights would suit her office and resolved to buy some, as well as an indoor plant, on the weekend.

"Poppy?" Mitch's head poked into Poppy's office interrupting her moment of peace. "Sorry, a customer needs help using Google translate on their phone. But their phone is all in French—which they don't speak. You speak French don't you?"

Poppy shook her head. "Nope, sorry." The service bell pinged in the background. *It must be busy out there. Oh well, a five-minute lunch is better than no lunch.* "I'll be out to help in a second." Poppy nodded for Mitch to head back out onto the floor. Putting her salad down, she drew in a deep breath and exhaled as the bell rang again. *Yep, I could definitely do with some Lykke in my life.*

The hallway security light flickered as Poppy, weary from an afternoon of moving shelving and troubleshooting self-service machines, turned the key in the front door of her rental apartment. She dropped her bag onto the mission brown linoleum floor and reached for the kettle. *Tea makes everything better*, she yawned, hopeful that a strong brew would lift her spirits. A one-hour ride on a standing room only bus was enough to break any hardened commuter. Dangling two proper strong tea bags into her mug, Poppy cringed. Next door was at it again. They were louder tonight. Carl and Sven's signature song thumped—something about 'you make me horny' and 'come on big boy'. It was going to be a late night for everyone.

Staring wishfully at the cutout magazine pictures she'd stuck to the fridge, Poppy did her best to focus on the hum of boiling water and slip into the images of country Australia brightening her kitchen. The photos from articles about people who'd packed up everything and moved to the great outdoors warmed her heart. *One day,* she sighed. *It'd be so satisfying to collect chicken eggs and then cook them in a cozy country kitchen.*

Poppy had been scrimping and saving to buy herself her own piece of paradise. The only money she'd really spent on herself, in the last two years, was on a meditation retreat and a new pair of glasses with icicle pink frames. The rims had been colour matched to the small geometric tattoo of a lotus bloom inked on the inside of her wrist—a personal reminder that, even from the darkest of places, beautiful things can grow. Poppy had applied for every country librarian position that had been advertised. Made phone calls to people she'd met at conferences and networked to headache inducing standards. So far, she'd had no luck. More and more she found herself dreading the early morning public transport commute to the inner-city library her sister always joked was her home.

'Your customers see more of you than we do, sis!'

It was true. Almost as true as the other MacLuster family joke that the only men that got a chance to lust over Poppy were the ones aged sixty and beyond. To which, she replied haughtily that libraries weren't just for the retired. Poppy knew she didn't have any work-life balance. Heck! She could even be classed as a born-again-virgin it'd been that long.

Lost in the romance of one day owning bantam hens, Poppy forgot about the steam that was now spewing into the room. The smoke alarm screamed and shocked her back to her linoleum shoebox of a reality. She lunged for the broom...

"Fu... bugger bloody bum!" Poppy cradled her foot and held back tears. *Damn.* She pressed the end of the broom handle into the alarm and flicked the power button on the jug. With ringing ears and a throbbing toe, she eyed the offending, now strewn, pile of books—information about straw bale houses and permaculture design. *I bet every country cottage has a bookshelf.* She pouted momentarily, before being shocked again by a banging on the door.

Poppy opened the door and stood wide-eyed in front of a scantily clad Sven.

"You alright Love?" Sven frowned. "I heard beeping, then banging."

Sven's bare belly hung over his hibiscus-covered sarong. His fuzzy grey chest glistened in the hallway light. Poppy suspected coconut oil. The corners of her mouth lifted. "Having a nice evening, then Sven?"

"Well, you know Carl likes a party," Sven winked. Poppy didn't miss the way his eyes glistened when he mentioned his partner of thirty years.

She could only hope that one day she would share a love like theirs.

"Yeah, I'm all good, thanks Sven. I let the kettle boil over and it set off the alarm. Again. Then I stubbed my toe. I think I'm just going to have a cuppa and head to Bedfordshire."

"You know it's Thursday night, love? Shouldn't you be hitting some trendy cocktail bar? Librarians are hot real estate these days. Carl and I were only saying this afternoon you need to meet yourself a nice young fella." Sven's concern for her sex life and heart was endearing, but Poppy didn't have the strength to discuss her non-orgasmic existence. Not wanting to be rude, she fought back a yawn. Tears filled her eyes.

"Alright love, I'll leave it. You look exhausted. And I can't make promises Carl can't keep, but we'll try to keep it down. Hey, how did your community garden proposal go?"

She loved how Sven was genuinely interested. "It went well, but it wasn't their vision..." Poppy stopped at what she thought was Carl cat-whistling from inside their apartment.

Sven winked. "Sorry, love. Gotta go."

"No worries," Poppy smiled, secretly wishing it were she being called back to the bedroom for something steamier than a hot beverage. *At least some people in the building are living their best life.*

Poppy locked the door behind her and resigned her attention to the task of making tea. She watched the hot water in her mug swirl into a strong brew. The smell of the dark leaves permeated the room. Bar a few feint giggles, everything was quiet once again.

CHAPTER 2

"You want me to what?" Poppy sat statue-like, in front of the newly appointed director of Sydney's city libraries, Daniel Stringer, conjuring the image of her lotus tattoo and trying not to lose her calm. Behind him, a glass wall revealed a sprawl of high-rises and bitumen that stretched out as far as the eye could see. The public library was on street level and Poppy had never been this high in the building before. She felt nauseous. Although, she had to admit, the overuse of aftershave and the shiny, slicked-back and overly dyed, black head of hair before her brought a somewhat comedic tone to an otherwise serious situation. *I bet this guy's never done a day of manual work in his life. Or actually met any of our customers. Or worked in an actual library.* Poppy's mind rampaged. Screw being Zen, she wanted to sucker-punch him.

"We want you to move up from library supervisor to team leader. You'll get an extra ten thousand dollars in pay and you'll have the advantage of managing the transition into the new tech hub."

"But what about the books?" Poppy struggled to gather her breath and thoughts. Surely, she was dreaming. It couldn't be right. The suggestion was ludicrous.

"The what?" The man Poppy would forever more refer to as 'Bloody Bastard' looked bewildered.

Poppy wanted to scream. *THE BOOKS. You know the things with covers and pages with words on them. Where are they going to go if we bring in all this tech stuff? What about the meeting spaces and comfy chairs? And seriously, what's wrong with the word 'library'?* But all she could do was sit there and turn an embarrassingly obvious shade of beetroot.

"The chairs will stay," said Bloody Bastard as if reading her mind. "Sitting areas meet the Mayor's agenda for creating inclusive spaces for the elderly." Poppy wondered if he knew that eighty percent of their elderly customers, the ones who 'needed' to sit, were basically allergic to using technology in an anaphylactic way. It still amazed her that some people got by, albeit just, without email. "You either want the promotion or not," Bloody Bastard continued. "You know you're the best person for the job. You have the experience. You're great with customers and the juniors."

YOU. YOU. YOU. Poppy raged, her calm having well and truly left. How could he know she knew all the regular's names and their reading preferences and that she drew a strong crowd to every children's story time? He'd barely been there long enough to make an espresso in his fancy office *'it's Italian darling,'* coffee machine. Poppy doubted he'd ever read a book from cover to cover in his life. "You mean, I have the perfect smile for convincing customers that getting rid of their library and replacing it with what will be the city's biggest technological hub is a good thing?"

"Come on. Everyone here knows you are the librarian version of Roald Dahl's Miss Honey." Poppy's back stiffened. She squared her glasses and flattened her liberty pattern delphine skirt. *Miss Honey is damn awesome, thank you very much.* "The customers and staff love you. If you lead this change, the complaints will be minimal. And yes! You won't be a librarian anymore. You'll be Team Leader of Digital Innovation. But is that so bad?" Poppy could have knocked 'Bloody Bastard's' rolling eyes straight out of their sockets.

"Ye..." she started.

"I'll give you the weekend to think about it," Bloody Bastard interrupted. "But really, between you and me, this is the direction we are going. You either want a job or not." Poppy watched Bloody Bastard stand and tap the pile of official-looking papers that towered on his desk. "You have until Monday to tell me your decision.

The restructure is happening, Poppy. And look, I'd hate for this to ruin our friendship," he smooched. *The nerve. Friendship my butt.*

It was taking all of Poppy's meditation training not to let emotion overcome her and fall into a teary heap. "Thank you. Daniel. I'll let you know on Monday," she replied calmly, ignoring the way he undressed her with his eyes. *Ugh! Seriously. The man thinks he's God's gift to libraries and women.*

Taking his stack of official papers, 'Bloody Bastard' crossed the room to open the large mahogany door that closed his office. He stood in the open doorway as if waiting for Poppy to follow him. "I look forward to your response." He smiled all too confidently, signalling he was done with their conversation.

Poppy wanted to slap the smugness from his sexy grin but thought better of it. Instead, she nodded and followed the man, who was about swan off and ruin her professional life, across the foyer toward an open lift.

"Are you coming down?" 'Bloody Bastard' offered, before stepping into the lift and pressing the button that closed its doors.

"No. Thank you. I'll take the stairs," replied Poppy matter of fact.

"No worries. I'll hear from you on Monday then. Oh, and can you make sure there is tea for this afternoon's visit? The Mayor likes earl grey with lemon."

"Yep. It's ready to go." Poppy smiled as 'Bloody Bastard's' face disappeared. "We set up the tea station yesterday after we installed all the new self-serve machines," she added under her breath.

Poppy stood at the top of the stairwell, inhaling and exhaling rhythmically. Old receipts and bits of notepaper crinkled as she fumbled through her handbag. Her head thumped. How was she going to break it to Mitch and the other staff that their much-loved workplace and library was being turned into what would eventually look like something out of a sci-fi movie? And how was she going to explain to her regulars that soon the books would be moved off site into something that could only be described as a graveyard for what Bloody Bastard considered ancient relics? Poppy knew she didn't want the job, but the pay rise would mean she could save more money and faster build a deposit for a down payment on a piece of rural heaven. It pained her to admit she'd have to accept the new position.

A hint of silver foil glistened under the envelope she'd shoved into her bag yesterday. *Thank God.* Breaking open the packet of painkillers, Poppy knocked back two white tablets. Taking a gulp from her drink bottle, she turned the envelope over. A tiny image of a quaint cottage surrounded by leafy trees was stamped above the words Derrin Shire Council. *Never heard of the place.* Poppy slid her neatly manicured fingernail under the lip of the envelope just as her phone buzzed. It was Mitch. "Hey, what's up?"

"Our self-serve machines aren't working and one of the casuals has called in sick."

"Okay, I'm leaving the Director's office now. I'll be downstairs soon." Poppy hung up and shoved the envelope back into her bag. She made a mental note to open it later. *It's probably just more promotional material my cramped office can do without.*

Mitch pounced as soon as she emerged on the ground floor. "I'm so glad you're here!"

"Why? What's happened?" Mitch's desperation worried Poppy.

"The marketing team just posted to Facebook. Is it true?"

"Is what true?" Surely 'Bloody Bastard' hadn't ordered a press release on the new tech hub already?

"The space... the books... the..." Mitch stammered.

It was true. And judging by Mitch's shocked expression, Poppy knew the tension in her face revealed it well.

"What does this mean, for us, Poppy? Am I going to lose my job?" he asked melodramatically.

"No. No. You won't lose your job. You'll be fine, absolutely fine. We'll all be fine." Poppy cleared her throat. She knew she was reassuring herself as much as she was Mitch. She had no idea how much Bloody Bastard was telling the truth. How she was going to break the news to the rest of the staff who'd be arriving in less than fifteen minutes, Poppy hadn't a clue. "Gosh, I'm so sorry, Mitch. I just found out myself. I bet that's why the Mayor is visiting today."

"Will the media be here?" he asked rather excitedly for someone whose world was apparently coming to an end.

"Knowing Blo... I mean, Daniel, yes. He'll want to take any opportunity he can get to promote the new hub. And himself, for that matter." Poppy knew it was unprofessional to talk about her boss negatively, in front of the staff, but she was livid with the way 'Bloody Bastard' had manipulated her. She could see now that he had always planned on her saying yes to his offer. He knew she wouldn't let her customers or team down.

Poppy did her best to centre herself. She concentrated on the sensation of her stomach rising and falling. The forlorn faces of ten staff members stared back at her. The only person who looked remotely impressed by the news that the library was going to be rebranded the city's premier digital innovation hub was Gabby—a new Swedish employee who was visiting on a university exchange work placement, barely twenty-one years old and blushed every time Bloody Bastard's name was mentioned.

"So," Poppy concluded, "we will stay on here as staff and assist in the fit-out of the new machines, devices, scanners, computers, tablets, coding lab and 3D printers. Once we have launched as the Digital Innovation Hub, we will undergo training to skill ourselves with how to assist customers using the technology and be expected to welcome our new role. Any questions?"

Merle, the library's longest serving staff member, piped up. "What if someone wants to borrow a book?" Her concern was obvious.

Poppy forced a smile. "Yes. Well. They still can. For physical books, we will reserve it for them and the book they want will come from storage and be delivered here for them to pick up."

Mitch's eyebrows farrowed. "But they won't be able to browse the shelves?" he asked, "because there will be none, yeah?"

"They will be able to browse the digital shelves, and library 'e' collection, on the self-serve touch screen Discovery Catalogue—Daniel's naming, not mine—and download a book to a tablet or iPad." Poppy was met with blank expressions—minus of course Gabby who nodded far too enthusiastically and mentioned for the fourth time this being a great idea.

"What if they don't have one? A tablet thingy, I mean," Merle piped up again. "Not everyone does."

Poppy agreed with the anger she felt filling the staff room. "Look everyone, our library space has been chosen for this and if we want our jobs, we're going to have to find a way to make it work. I really am sorry you weren't all given any warning about this. I only found out about it myself this morning."

Poppy felt the daggers flying at her. She knew she sounded like one of them—someone who fed workers rote-phrases that sounded great but didn't address the elephant in the room. The one that was stomping and screaming *'THIS SUCKS'*.

Not knowing how she was going to wrap up the meeting positively, Poppy was relieved when the library's opening timer sounded. "Okay everyone. Well, um, enjoy your morning and I will see you all in the foyer this afternoon when the Mayor visits," she said with a forced smile. "Mitch can you please open the doors and let the customers in?"

The team dispersed. Poppy held her stomach and took a few more deep breaths. With the look of dejection on everyone's faces, she knew how upset they all were. Well, everyone apart from Gabby, of course, who Poppy assumed must be loving knowing that Bloody Bastard would be spending more time in the library being filmed and photographed for media releases.

Poppy closed the door to the library workroom and scrounged through her handbag for more painkillers. Did she really want to be Team Leader of the new Digital Innovation Hub? Could she say no to the extra pay? It wasn't as if she was rolling in it. Just then, the bottom of her bag buzzed.

"Hey sis. How's it going?" Poppy could hear the commotion. She wondered why it was that whenever Rachel rang, it always sounded like a rave for three-year-olds on the other end of the phone.

"Yeah... going well," Rachel coughed. "Chris is at work today, so I'm not up to much other than crowd control. Ben's got a play date happening with his friends. PUT THAT DOWN," Poppy held the phone in the air. If anyone could deafen her thirty-two-year-old ears instantaneously, it was Rachel. "Seriously, who created these monsters? I don't know. So, how's your day going, Pops?"

"Um. Well. Interesting. Stressful. And now I have to decide if I want to be Team Leader of Sydney's new Digital Innovation Hub."

"That's unexpected. Congratulations! Everyone say congratulations Aunty Pops." A chorus of little voices and squeals rang down the phone before Rachel got down to business. "The what? And do you get a pay rise?"

"Yes to a pay rise—an extra ten thousand—and I'll be Team Leader of the new Digital Innovation Hub," Poppy repeated. "The library is going to be the city's new tech hub. We just found out today. It's being filled with flashy stuff that I know not much about. They say that the library building is the perfect spot because it's near the art gallery and museums and, basically, it will look cool and state-of-the art to tourists," Poppy explained flatly.

"That's fantastic," said Rachel, trying to sound genuine. Poppy could always tell she was distracted by the way she paused in the middle of words, somewhat like a new age yoga teacher but way less relaxed.

"Is it? They are getting rid of, well moving, all the books and I won't be a librarian anymore." Poppy's heart sank at the thought.

"Oh Poppy!" exasperated Rachel, sounding somewhat fed-up. "They are paying you an extra ten thousand dollars per year. You can put that to your country dream or whatever."

Poppy felt the tears well. "But I feel like a sell out. I'll hate it. And no-one here agrees with it."

"Oh my God. Let's face it, Sis. Can you even see yourself moving to the country? BOYS. STOP. CLIMBING. The dust. The lack of water. The nothing to do. PUT THAT DOWN. NOW. I just want to see you settle down and be happy, Poppy. Meet a nice man and get out of that shoebox you call a flat and away from your party prone neighbours. BEN. I MEAN IT."

Poppy knew that Rachel, a city girl through and through, would never understand her desire to have fresh air in her lungs and toes curled in the grass. Rachel's idea of Poppy's happiness looked suspiciously the vision of a soccer mum. But nothing about Poppy wanted the latest SUV, fashion accessory or hairstyle. She'd much rather a car she didn't have to stress about, a pair of gum boots, and to let her natural long brown locks grow in whatever way they chose. Yet Poppy knew there was truth to Rachel's argument. The pay rise would equal welcome savings. For a woman of thirty-two, apart from people who loved her and a pile of travel photos collected in her early twenties, Poppy didn't have much to show for her life. She had always given money away to friends in need and charity projects, feeling grateful that she was educated enough to land on her own two feet. Although, being generous did mean that Poppy didn't have the biggest bank account in the world, she had always felt rich in other ways. But maybe things needed changing. "I love you heaps sis and I don't expect you to understand. But I hear what you're saying. And you are right, the money is important. I do need to think about setting myself up for the future."

"Hallelujah! Poppy, this is a great opportunity. It's not the country but now that you'll be earning more we can go out to the Highlands for girl's trips. I'll leave Chris to look after Ben. I need some alone time."

"Rachel, you have alone time every other day while Chris is at work and Ben is in day-care."

"Yeah but it's not relaxing is it? I always have so much to do."

"Like getting the shellac on your nails re-done and your roots dyed," Poppy jested.

"Haha. Very funny. Geez, I've got to go. Ben's climbing on the kitchen bench again and the housemaid will be here any minute. Love you and congratulations! I can't wait to tell my friends at Pilates about your promotion."

As much as she hated it, Poppy knew Rachel was right. She'd have to take the promotion regardless of whether she wanted it. She hated the thought of Daniel Bloody Bastard's smug *I knew you would* expression greeting her on Monday morning.

Poppy sighed and pressed her hand against her forehead. She couldn't remember the last time she had felt her jaw unclench. Reaching once again into her handbag, she pulled out the painkillers, and, with it, the white envelope from Derrin Shire Council. Taking a seat at her desk she swallowed the little tablets and slid open the envelope's seal. Poppy's heart thumped. Her hands shook. She couldn't believe what she was reading.

Dear Miss MacLuster,

On behalf of Derrin Shire Council, it gives me great pleasure to offer you the position of Head Librarian at Derrin Country Library. We thank you for your application and apologise for the delay in replying to your expression of interest. As you are aware, the position is contracted for 3 months starting on the 1st of July. Details of your remuneration and living package are included with this letter.

Derrin Country Library is set in the heart of a small, vibrant community that is home to just over 900 residents. If you choose to accept this position, you will be tasked with coordinating the library's services and programs; as well as, overseeing the maintenance of the surrounding buildings and gardens.

Please notify us of your acceptance of this position by 20th June COB. We look forward to hearing from you.

Kind regards,

Ms. Shirley Baxter

Human Resources Manager

Human Resources Department

Derrin Shire Council

Poppy felt her blood pressure plummet. She looked

at the calendar. The twentieth was... *TODAY.* She snapped open her laptop and searched for Derrin. Images of maple trees, quiet country roads, dairy farms, and quaint country buildings began to appear on the screen. It was the postcard perfect country life that Poppy had always dreamed of.

Lost in her utopia, Poppy barely heard the workroom door nudged open. It was Gabby.

"The Mayor is here. He's early. Daniel is taking care of things, of course," she gushed.

There must be at least fifteen years age difference between them calculated Poppy. She wondered why someone as young and attractive as Gabby would be falling for a womaniser. Maybe she hadn't heard on the grapevine that 'Bloody Bastard' was a man who had a penchant for international 'cuisine' and was eating his way around the world one woman at a time. Or that he'd been forced to move on from his last job after cheating on his then fiancé with the office trainee—a young lady from London.

"Poppy?" Gabby paused. "Are you coming? Mitch has served the tea. Daniel said the Mayor is going to give a speech."

"A speech? What about?" In their meeting this morning, Daniel hadn't mentioned anything about a speech.

"Not sure. All I know is the media are here and you're going to miss it if you don't come now."

Daniel 'Bloody Bastard' Stringer swooned beside the Mayor of Sydney and his staff. His cocky stature was absolutely nauseating. Poppy wondered if she'd ever have to encounter someone as smug as Daniel in Derrin. It was a nice thought not to. But how could she accept the offer with only half a day to think about it? Could she really risk everything for three months in the country? What about her apartment? Her family? What about the people she worked with—what would happen to them? Surely, she couldn't say yes, then pack up and move to a new life in the country in ten days, with only the promise of a few months being the total sum of her known professional future? The idea was ridiculous. Wasn't it?

'Bloody Bastard' clinked his teacup. The mumbles silenced as the team and lingering customers turned to face the Mayor.

"Good afternoon. Ah, thank you everyone for joining us here this morning. Firstly, I'd like to acknowledge the Traditional Owners of the land upon which the new Digital Innovation Hub will stand." Camera lights flashed. The Mayor's team 'oohed' and 'aahed'. A man with thick long chords trailing from his arms and a microphone on his shoulder brushed past Poppy, without so much as an excuse me. "As you all know, we have a long and positive history of working to progress the needs of this city and its community. Last year, we hit the ground running, asking people what they wanted from their city library. Well, we listened, and the new Digital Innovation Hub is our answer. Now, I know what you may be thinking, Digital Innovation Hub, does it really cater to what people are asking for? We say 'yes'!" The Mayor's white teeth flashed and his staff applauded. Poppy waited for someone to hand the man a baby. "Now is the time for me to stand up as your Mayor and deliver on promises to take our city into the future." Another pause. More clapping. "But, rest assured, this will still be the community haven you've all come to love. Not only will you be able to borrow all your beloved books in electronic format, you will also be able to relax with a coffee in our new café before wandering through the outdoor learning garden—a feature that has just been agreed upon, this morning, and is thanks to our new idea's man and director, Daniel Stringer.

Poppy's jaw dropped.

"IDEAS MAN. That bloody swine. His idea? His idea!" Poppy paced between the office computers in the library workroom. "I cannot believe it. I knew it was a great idea but when Daniel said 'no' I didn't expect that he was secretly saying 'yes, I love it and I'll take the idea for my own' What an arse..."

Poppy had been ranting to Mitch non-stop for the last fifteen minutes. He nodded in empathetic agreement. "It's true, Poppy. He flat out stole ya idea but what are ya gonna do about it?"

"I'm going up there!" exclaimed Poppy looking possessed.

"Where?"

Mitch's blank express told Poppy he thought she'd lost the plot. She didn't care.

"*There*." She lifted her finger to the ceiling. "I'm going straight to his office."

"Poppy. No. Wait. Shouldn't ya calm down first? I mean don't say anything you'd regret. Remember all the woo-woo stuff you're always talking about— 'responding, not reacting'; 'breath before bitch'—-it's a great time to use it." Poppy admired the way Mitch tried to prevent her from doing something he thought she might later regret.

"Thank you, Mitch. For a junior, you show great maturity. But I can't accept the position of Team Leader of this new hub if I can't trust that Daniel isn't going to take every good idea I have and pass it off as his own. I'll be back soon." Resolved, Poppy picked up her handbag and headed out the workroom door.

Bloody Bastard's mahogany office door looked more pretentious than ever. Poppy could have sworn she heard giggles coming from the other side of it. Uncaring, she used the reflection in the shiny gold-plated name plaque to flatten her peter pan collar, smooth her bun and tuck a brown escapee tendril behind her ear. And then, she knocked.

Silence. Clearing of the throat.

"Um. Yes. Who is it?"

"It's Poppy."

"Come in. My meeting is finishing up."

Daniel looked calm, cool and collected, when Poppy entered his office. What was shocking was seeing Gabby there too. Poppy's eyes darted between the two faces before her. *Breath before bitch, breath before bitch...* she chanted.

"Gabby shouldn't you be working on catalogue maintenance in the biography section?" Poppy could barely get the question out. Surely there was a logical reason for Gabby giggling in 'Bloody Bastard's' office.

"Daniel asked me to bring up his mobile," blushed Gabby.

Daniel puffed his chest out and stepped forward. "I left it downstairs after saying goodbye to the Mayor. Foolish of me. What can I help you with, Poppy?"

Foolish or calculating? wondered Poppy. *Does the man have no morals?* She had seen the way he'd glanced at Gabby during the Mayor's speech–it was the same way he'd glanced at her earlier that morning. Poppy opened her mouth in answer, only to be interrupted by Gabby's Scandinavian chirpiness. "I'll be seeing you later then, Daniel?" she flirted, as she left the room, flicking her blonde hair and turning back for one last glance.

"Ahem, yes. Yes. I'll be down at 5 o'clock for that thank you drink," replied 'Bloody Bastard', sounding every bit like an obnoxious Hugh Grant. Poppy could have sworn she saw Gabby wink.

With the door now closed, Poppy focused her attention on the reason she was there in the first place. "Daniel, I'm here to talk to you about the Mayor's speech."

"Oh yes. Boring wasn't it? They all are though."

Poppy felt herself go blotchy with anger. "I found the bit about the learning garden quite interesting, actually."

"Great idea isn't it. I can't remember who came up with it but I think it'll work well and it will meet the requirement for us to provide green space."

Great idea! Provide green space! How could he be so blasé about ripping off her idea as his own? She had pitched it with a spreadsheet and PowerPoint presentation, for heck's sake! "I know very well how great the idea is, Daniel, because it was mine."

"Oh, was it? That's right. You pitched it at one of

our meetings," Bloody Bastard said, infuriatingly nonchalantly.

Poppy gritted her teeth. "Yes, and you basically said it didn't meet any future requirements for the library."

"Yes. But then the Mayor mentioned the hub having to meet environmental standards for providing natural spaces within the city centre and asked how that would be achieved. That's when I said we had an idea to turn the paved unused courtyard area out the back into a vibrant community garden for locals to meet and learn new hands-on skills. Gabby is going to manage the project. Apparently, she's got quite the green thumb. Used to be a florist in Stockholm, or something."

"Gabby!" Poppy choked. "But it was *my* idea. And she's an exchange student!"

"You won't have time to look after the creation of the garden if you're leading the Digital Innovation Team, will you?" Bloody Bastard shrugged. "And it will be a great professional development opportunity for Gabby."

Poppy wanted to scream. She wanted to cry. She wanted to stomp her feet and yell *IT'S MY BLOODY IDEA YOU BLOODY BASTARD*. She could no longer hear what 'Bloody Bastard' was saying—something about needing fresh eyes for a fresh project, collaborating ideas, IKEA and Scandinavian's always being so cutting edge. Caught in her fury, Poppy saw her life flash before her eyes. Life as a singleton in a beige—almost baby-poo coloured city apartment with a collection of cats, she didn't even want, all named after Harry Potter characters —life as someone who had sold their dreams for money and now spent Friday nights scrolling through Instagram wonder-lusting over people who were actually living enough to have photographic evidence.

NO. NO. NO. Poppy started to hyperventilate. She couldn't. Wouldn't. In a moment that she would later describe to Rachel as *sanely insane*—a type of moment where one might think the spirit of some wild and free hippy possessed them—Poppy did something she never thought she would do. She told Daniel Bloody Bastard Stringer to shove it.

CHAPTER 3

"What have you done?!"

Poppy couldn't work out if Rachel was angry or plain furious. "I've quit. Well, I'm taking all my leave first, but yes, I quit. Oh and I'm moving to Derrin. I start there in ten days," Poppy replied matter of fact, holding her mobile against her ear with one hand and shoving clothes into a suitcase with another.

What am I going to do with all this stuff? Poppy wondered as she wrapped another deer statue in tissue paper.

"Where the hell *is* Derrin? Is it an outer suburb or something?"

Poppy couldn't understand why it was so hard for her sister to support her. She'd wanted to move to the country since she was a child and now it was happening, albeit for only three glorious months. "It's about a three-hour train journey into the Southern Highlands. Google told me it's quite picturesque."

I'm going to have to put all of this into a storage unit.

"Does Google know you are packing up your life and moving to the middle of nowhere to work in an old decrepit building and give up a ten thousand dollar pay rise for a few months of work?"

"It might," said Poppy with as much sarcasm as she could muster. "And the library is not decrepit. It's an opportunity. Hey speaking of packing up. Can I store a few boxes in your garage?"

"Ha. Ha." The flatness of Rachel's voice made it obvious to Poppy that Rachel would not agree with her anytime soon. Not that it was her sister's decision, but Poppy really wanted Rachel to feel happy for her. She wanted her to understand how excited she was. This was the fresh start Poppy needed.

"I'm serious. I'm only taking one suitcase with me. The new place is fully furnished. It's called Page Cottage, isn't that the cutest? I'll only need to store a couple of boxes, I swear." Rachel sighed down the phone. Poppy took this as confirmation that she was finally getting through to her sister. "Look, this is a really great opportunity for me. I get to do what I love. I have a house ready and waiting for when I arrive. My pay won't be too much less than it is now, and I won't have to put up with smug idiots like Daniel. He seemed put out when I quit but quickly reminded me that what I did was replaceable and he would find someone else equally capable, I reckon his ego took a beating, though. So much for me being the only one who could take the promotion and win over the customers."

"That sucks. But what about the people you work with? Your team? What about... us?"

Poppy heard Rachel's voice crack. She felt bad for leaving her sister and family. Her workmates had been shocked at her resignation. But she was only moving three hours away and there was a train service to the town.

Shutting down the guilt that was stabbing at her, Poppy reassured her sister that, if needed, she could come back at the drop of a hat and that she and Ben could visit whenever they wanted. "You have Chris and it'd be great to have you guys over once I'm settled, it's not like I'm moving to the other side of the world. Ben would love the country, I'm sure. Who knows, I might even get some chickens." Rachel was silent on the other end of the phone.

Poppy knew she would miss the people she had worked with for such a long time. Mitch had been upset by the news. He thought it abrupt, and Poppy couldn't blame him for feeling abandoned. The only people that had seemed truly happy for her had been Sven and Carl, who'd both shed tears of joy when she had told them she would sub-let her flat for a few months and be moving to the greener pastures for a while.

"Come on Rach. I really want you to be happy for me and it's not for long."

"But, I, I..." The tears began to flow. "I'm going to miss you."

"Aw, come on now. I'm going to miss you too, but I'm not that far away, really." Poppy tried her best to console Rachel, while single-handedly wrestling with the zip on her bulging suitcase.

"I guess," Rachel sniffled. "But it's just so quick. I mean, on Monday you'll be off."

"Yeah, crazy, isn't it? I can't believe it. All those applications I filled in and had no reply and now I've landed my dream job. I don't even care that it's only for three months. I'm just so excited—I get a cute little cottage with a garden and fresh air. Genuine fresh country air." Poppy smiled at the sound of Rachel's chuckle. "So can I store some boxes in your garage?"

"You cheeky beggar. Yeah, go on then. A few will be okay and Chris won't mind—actually, he works so much these days he probably won't notice. How about Ben and I come around on Sunday and pick them up for you?"

"Oh Rach, you're a gem. That'd be great. And thanks for understanding. I promise I haven't gone bat crap bonkers."

"I don't understand. And I *do* think you've gone

bonkers. But if this decision makes you happy I guess I shouldn't try to stop you."

Poppy smiled. "It does make me happy. Very."

Poppy surveyed the bedroom that was soon to be someone else's. She would not miss the orange wallpaper and brown shag-pile carpet. When she first moved in, Poppy thought the décor trendy in a retro way, but now she was just looking forward to waking up to a colour that didn't remind her of some form of faeces. She was grateful to Sven for offering to look after the subletting of her apartment. With everything else to do, it was a great relief to know that she didn't have to sort out tenants. She really didn't care who lived in it, only that it wasn't destroyed when she got back.

Excitement bubbled inside her. Poppy had lived in the city her entire life but had never truly felt at home in the concrete jungle. She always sought out the quieter greener parts of the neighbourhood, cobble stone streets, back alleys where vines grew, and secret gardens. Every Sunday, after yoga, Poppy would sit in the Chinese Friendship Gardens, with a cup of tea and pretend she was far away, surrounded by open paddocks and leafy hideaways. Her grandmother always said a tree was a man's best friend and she couldn't agree more.

Poppy had tried to remind Rachel of this yesterday

as they piled the packed moving boxes into the back of her car. It hadn't worked. Rachel had still been overly emotional and Poppy couldn't help but wonder why. Was there something more going on than Rachel had been letting on? Her sister was usually so supportive, and it had surprised Poppy that Rachel was still trying to convince her to stay.

Poppy's mobile pinged. Her UBER was five minutes away. Rolling her only suitcase behind her, she said goodbye to the space she had spent far too many Friday nights alone in. Breathing in gratitude for the chance at a new life, she closed the door behind her.

Poppy smiled and brushed the light pink lotus on the inside of her right wrist. This was it. This was the moment she started living.

CHAPTER 4

"Derrin. Derrin Station."

Poppy snapped back to reality. She hoped no one had noticed the drool escaping from the corners of her mouth.

"Derrin. Derrin Station."

The train carriage was all but empty. There had been few people on the last service. It was only herself and a couple of older men left on the train. Dressed in checkered flannelette shirts, leather boots and Akubra hats, they looked like they'd come straight from a rodeo. Muttering something about cattle sales and the price of steers, they brushed past. Poppy waited for them to exit before she proceeded to the baggage cage.

The station could have belonged on a tea tin. Two small, wooden clad buildings, painted in duck egg blue, edged the tracks. Rosemary bushes glistened in the warm glow of Victorian style street lamps. Their woody stems formed neat hedges between the buildings and crusher dust paths. The air smelt different—herby and fresh, with a hint of eucalypt. Poppy filled her lungs with its frostiness and felt the smog clear from her veins.

Darkness had already begun to fall over the Highlands as the train had made its way out of the city's outer suburbs. Winter's frosted landscape had emerged only briefly before the last of the day's fading light. There was something very romantic about arriving in a new place at night, thought Poppy, as she zipped her tartan trench coat to her neck and reached into her bag.

Fumbling around with numb fingers, trying to locate her mobile phone, she reminded herself to buy mittens as soon as she could. *There you are.*

No reception. Nothing. *Bugger.*

Poppy had promised to text Rachel as soon as the train pulled into Derrin. She had no idea that phone reception would be a problem. Not to mention all the instructions for getting to her new home, Page Cottage, were in her phone's email app.

"Excuse me." Poppy waved eagerly at a tall man who strode down the footpath on the other side of the road. The glow from the streetlights highlighted his muscular physique. If it weren't for Poppy fearing that her toes might turn to icicles, she may have been nervous approaching someone who looked as though they could easily pick her up and fling her over their shoulder. Fighting against the cold air, she forced her lips upward. "Sorry, but do you know why there isn't any phone service here?" she smiled as she crossed the road to join him. If he was a local, she wanted to make a good impression. He wore a flannelette shirt and leather boots. Poppy wondered if it was some sort of town uniform she didn't know about.

"You with Telstra?" the man replied, breathing frost from his chiseled jaw. He stood, hands rigid in his jeans pockets, looking put out that she had attracted his attention.

"No, I'm not, but it's not usually a problem. I get reception just fine in the city."

"Well, you ain't in the city anymore, are you?" he answered coolly. Poppy watched his dark brown eyes fall to her pink kitten heal pumps causing her to feel completely overdressed. Her skin grew hot.

"No, I guess, I'm not." Poppy wondered if she had in some way offended him. She also wondered how she would find her way to the cottage, once she knew where it was, in the freezing cold dark, with a suitcase in hand and no access to the maps app on her phone. This wasn't starting well.

"If you want reception, you're going to have to change your carrier." The man crossed his arms and pushed his shirtsleeves up to his elbows as if it were summer. Poppy couldn't help but notice how the veins pulsed down his forearms. "In the meantime, there's a phone in the pub at the end of this block," he added, pointing down the road.

"Are you going that way too? Monday night football and beers is it?" Poppy tried her best to be chirpy and forget about her choice of inappropriate footwear and phone service provider.

"I don't drink," he replied abruptly, before walking on into the night.

"Okay. Well, thanks for that," Poppy muttered after him. *I thought people in the country were supposed to be welcoming?*

The inside of the pub was a welcome sight. Although it smelt classically of spilt beer and lingering tobacco smoke, it was warm. An open fire raged in the corner of the cattlemen's bar. Taxidermised fish, bullhorns and stag heads hung on the walls. The menagerie was framed by photos of the area's pioneering history, visits by famous country music singers and rodeo cowboys. Near the bar was a set of French doors that swung open every few seconds, revealing a cozy restaurant where people helped themselves to a hot steamy buffet. The scent of gravy and roast vegetables hit Poppy's nostrils. Saliva filled her mouth.

Dropping her suitcase out of the way and against the wall, she walked over to the fire in desperate need to feel her cheeks, feet and fingers again. Her bones shook.

Poppy was amazed to see that so many people filled the space. She had imagined the pub empty considering that it was a Monday night and so few people had been outside on the street. Laughter echoed off the walls, pool cues clinked and country music danced around the tables. She looked around for someone who she could ask directions. The sooner she got out of her city clothes and into a hot shower, the better.

Walking over to the bar, Poppy noticed the man she had spoken to on the street sitting on a stool. The bright light revealed his tanned skin and dark hair. His strong hands wrapped around a pint glass and drew attention to the shirt that now tightened around his flexed biceps. Poppy's breath quickened as he took a long sip. They didn't make men like this in the city. He wasn't just good looking—he was a Calvin Klein model meets Jamie Fraser good looking. Feeling brave, Poppy perched next to him.

"I thought you didn't drink," she remarked cheerfully, trying to sound casual and not like a horny teenage schoolgirl.

The man didn't even look sideways. "This is soda water and bitters."

"Sounds refreshing. Although, I have to say it's pretty cold up this way. I think a hot chocolate would be better suited," Poppy added, trying to sound lighthearted.

"You're welcome to buy yourself one in the

restaurant," he gestured toward the French doors with a bluntness that clearly said, 'I don't want to talk to you'.

Poppy wondered why he had such a chip on his shoulder. Surely, he could tell she was only trying to be friendly. "I might do that later." She replied with a half-smile, ignoring his cool demeanour. She watched him wash down the last of his glass before he stood up and strode out the door without so much as acknowledging her. Poppy couldn't understand why this stranger's behaviour was offending her so much. *I mean, he's damn good-looking, but it's not like we know each other or anything. No wonder he's here alone.* Turning her attention to the young woman who had just ducked behind the bar, Poppy waved. "Excuse me. Do you know how to get to Page Cottage?"

"Sure do!" Poppy was relieved to finally have someone smile at her. The young woman looked about the same age as Poppy. Her fiery red hair was tied back with a lime green scarf and highlighted the nose ring that glistened against her right nostril. "I'm Veronica. But people around here call me 'Nica', for short. Is that your suitcase?" Nica's green eyes sparkled under the bar lights. Poppy watched as she darted from tap to tap. Her exuberance reminded Poppy of what a woodland fairy might look like with a couple of champers under her wings.

"Yes, it's mine. I'm Poppy." Poppy reached over the

bar and shook Nica's hand. "It's great to meet someone friendly."

"Don't worry about him. He's always tired and grumpy," she smiled. "So did you come in on the last train?"

Poppy watched Nica wipe down the bar and refill the complimentary snack bowls. "Yep. Just arrived, hence the suitcase. I don't have any phone reception to contact my family back in Sydney, and I'm not quite sure how to get to the cottage."

"From the big smoke, hey? Wowsers." Nica paused for a minute before pouring an order for four pints of Guinness. Poppy was in awe of her efficiency. "What brings you out here to Derrin?" she continued.

"A new job. I'm going to work at the library."

"Cool! We'll be neighbours. I run the pottery classes next door."

Poppy brimmed with excitement. "The library has an art studio?"

"Not as such. The library is the building beside us. It's in the same grounds. Which is a bit run down, mind, but there's a Men's Shed, the art space I mentioned and also a permaculture garden—but anyone would be forgiven for thinking it a weed patch. No one's really taken care of it. The nasturtiums have outgrown the cobblers pegs and are threatening to take over the entire complex. I'm planning on taking the secateurs with me this week, it's gotten so bad."

"You must have your hands full working here as well," remarked Poppy.

"Nah," replied Nica casually as she finished the pour on a Guinness. "I'm just filling in for Bob. He and Rose own and run this place. Bob came down with the man flu last week." Poppy couldn't help but giggle at the way Nica rolled her eyes. "And it's pretty busy this time of year with tourists. I told him I'd do a few shifts to help Rose while he recovers. I really have no idea what I'm doing. If I'm not volunteering at the community hub, you'll usually find me in my own art studio."

"You're an artist?" Poppy, who had barely mastered a stick figure, was genuinely impressed.

"She's a brilliant artist, our Nica." A short, plump woman with flour on her apron and a box of packaged nuts appeared from behind a closed door.

"You're too kind, Rose," said Nica, brushing off the compliment. "Rose is also the Head Chef."

"Just being honest, dear." Rose patted a blushing Nica on the shoulder. "Nica's got her work hanging in the local gallery. Sold one to a tourist the other day didn't you dear?" she added, before leaning over the bar and shaking Poppy's hand. "I'm Rose dear—'Jill of all trades'."

"Poppy. Nice to meet you—selling artworks, that's awesome. I'll have to have a look on my next day off." Poppy couldn't wait to immerse herself in some of the local culture.

"Let me know when you're keen. I'll meet you there," replied Nica as she balanced a tower of glasses in her arms.

"And what are you here for dear?" asked Rose. Poppy watched her push packets of salted peanuts onto a stand.

"Poppy's the new librarian and overseer of the community hub," interrupted Nica. "She's replacing Carmen."

"Speaking of, how do I get to Page Cottage? And would you mind terribly if I connected to your Wi-Fi? My sister will have the police looking for me, if I don't message her and tell her I've arrived. And I also need to order an UBER?"

"You'll be waiting a long time for an UBER," laughed Nica. "We don't have them here. But look for 'The Grand' in your Wi-Fi list. The password is 'morebeer'. As for getting to Page Cottage, I knock off in fifteen minutes. If you're happy to wait, I don't mind dropping you off on my way home."

"That would be wonderful. Gosh, I really do have some adjusting to do, don't I? No UBER."

"Why don't you take a seat over near the fire? There's a power point over there. You can plug your phone in, if it needs charging. I'll get Rose to bring you over some hot chips. On the house. You look like you could do with some warming up."

After a fairly lengthy conversation with Rachel, Poppy settled into an armchair next to the fireplace and absorbed the heat into her body. The flames lulled her into a quiet slumber as she began to feel her feet again. Her pumps looked out of place here, she thought. Nearly everyone was dressed in jeans, a collared shirt, and boots. Poppy looked down at her pleated, polka-dot skirt and grey tights. Five hours ago she'd thought herself stylish, but now she felt way over the top. She was glad she'd been able to get hold of Rachel, who'd taken a while to calm down after Poppy had broken it to her that she had been stranded for the last fifteen minutes without mobile phone reception. Rachel thought it positively archaic and demanded that Poppy return to the land of the living at once. The only thing that placated her was mentioning that she'd had a very brief conversation with a hot man. Poppy hadn't mentioned the bit about him being rude and practically ignoring her.

It was nearly nine-thirty in the evening, by the time Nica put the key into the ignition of the small bright yellow hatchback she called Bumblebee. The two of them chatted away as they pulled out of the main street and down a quiet dirt road. The rolling hills and sky blended into one dark abyss. Every so often, a house light glowed in the distance. The car's high beams lit up the tall grass on the side of the road and illuminated the odd escapee cow. The mist had begun to roll in. It looked cold outside. Poppy hoped there was a working heater in her new home.

"We'll be there in five minutes," said Nica.

"I didn't think the cottage was this far from town. It seems a lot further out than I thought."

"You city folk always think everything in the country is far away," Nica jested. "It's only a ten-minute drive. I just like to take the driving slower at night. You never know what critters are on the road. I'd hate to hit a hare. Deer can be pretty skittish, too."

"Deer! There are deer here?" Poppy squealed. Ever since she was a small child, they had fascinated her. Her flat back in Sydney had been adorned with all sorts of deer accessories. There was something about their majestic power that captivated her. There was nothing more impressive than a stag with fully grown antlers and Poppy couldn't wait to see one.

"There are heaps of deer here. Not everyone is as enthusiastic as you about them but you're sure to see one, or maybe even a few. They are out mostly in the mornings, evenings and nighttime. I once had this moment with a stag on my way to the art studio, one morning. I was feeling pretty low. My last boyfriend had unceremoniously dumped me by text message after he'd declared that I didn't earn enough money. I asked the universe for a sign that everything was going to be okay.

Next minute, I turned the corner and there's a stag standing to attention on the road with his chest out and antlers proudly on display. It caught my breath. It was the most beautiful thing I'd ever seen. He stared right through me, then casually walked off the road and leapt gracefully into the bushes. I swear he was sent to assure me that everything would be okay—that I should keep my head high and carry on with grace. So I did."

"Wow. That's an epic story. I can't believe he dumped you because of money. What a shallow idiot!" Poppy exclaimed incredulously. "That stag was definitely there to tell you that you deserve better. I love deer too. I've always had an affinity with them. My grandfather was a deer farmer. As a kid, I loved going with him to the deer sheds. Not that I was allowed in. There was always a lot of banging and swearing going on the other side of the walls. Sometimes he'd come out with the shirt ripped off his back and I'd secretly cheer on the deer that got the better of him." Poppy laughed remembering the many times her Granddad had come off second best.

"Hey. Are you going to the rodeo?"

"I didn't know there was one on. Is it a big event?"

"Yeah kind of. Everyone will be there and some from out of town too. You should come!"

"Sounds great. When is it?" Getting out and about was just what Poppy knew she needed. Being in Derrin was a chance at a new life; a chance to not be the person that spent most nights alone. Plus, she'd never been to a rodeo before and had read a lot about them.

"It's this coming Friday, you've arrived just in time. The library will be busy leading up to it. You wait. You'll have the cowboys and clowns coming in to use the public computers. Probably to check the hook-up apps, knowing half the boys on the circuit." Nica chuckled as if she knew them all too well. "Good guys though. They'll come into the bar, of course."

Bumblebee's engine gurgled down the narrow country roads. The sound of Nica chatting away beside her was making Poppy sleepy. She was just about to ask if they were far off arriving, when Bumblebee's headlights shone onto a signpost that pointed to Rose Lane. Poppy was instantly revived. She sat up in her seat, eager to catch the first glimpse of her new home.

"Nearly there!" Nica sounded as excited as Poppy felt. "It's just at the end of this road," she added as they turned into Rose Lane.

After driving through what Poppy had assumed was farmland, she was surprised to see two small farm cottages lining the left side of the dirt road.

"These houses have been here since the early 1900s," offered Nica. "It used to be one big dairy farm, until it was subdivided into the smaller house lots for family members. And of course, they've been sold on over the years. Here we are, your home sweet new home. Page Cottage." Nica slowed the car down and pulled into a gravel drive "You have keys, I presume?"

"Where's the cottage?" hesitated Poppy. She wondered if she should get out of the car or not. "It looks like a serial killer lives here." Bumblebee's headlights glowed into the dark and revealed a gardener's nightmare.

Nica's brow farrowed. "It's a bit overgrown isn't it? I'm sure the cottage is behind there somewhere."

Overgrown was an understatement. Vines and bushes coiled and tangled themselves over the front fence and trailed off into the depths of the night. Poppy's stomach turned.

"So do you have the keys?" repeated Nica.

"Not yet. They should be in the letterbox, hopefully. I remember that bit from one of the very first emails I received confirming my position. Since then, the communication has been non-existent, so I hope the keys are in there." Poppy said in a rather too high pitch that betrayed her efforts to seem confident.

"No hopefully about it. If they're meant to be in the letterbox, they'll be there. Half the people in this town don't even lock their doors. Plus, your neighbour is ultra safety conscious," Nica winked.

Poppy had no idea what Nica was winking for and wondered for a second if her new friend had an eye spasm. "What do you mean?"

"Oh nothing," she smiled. "Come on. I'll help you find the key."

Poppy was too cold and tired to probe any further. "Are you sure? You've already done so much." Poppy didn't mean a word of what she said. She was realising now just how nervous she was about being alone in what had begun to feel like a very scary place.

Nica, on the other hand, having been a local since birth, seemed completely at ease. "Of course! I'm not driving away until I know for sure that you've unlocked the door. Not that there are any axe murderers around here."

"I don't know. It looks pretty Sleepy Hollowish to me." Poppy wished she were joking.

Chuckling, Nica grabbed hold of Poppy's arm. "Come on. No point in freezing to death in the car."

Poppy tapped the torch app on her mobile phone. *The letterbox must be here somewhere?* She waved the light around the rambling-overgrown garden, trying to find a gate. *Letter boxes are always near gates.* She could hear the feint hum of voices coming from the other side of dense overgrowth that covered what looked like a mulberry tree and an old picket fence.

"This is a total Secret Garden moment, isn't it?" Nica said wide-eyed.

"I love how you think Secret Garden and not Stephen King. There!"

It wasn't a letterbox but the find still excited Poppy

who'd all but forgotten that, only a moment ago, she'd been freaked out by the sheer silence of the place. With a gentle push, the old gate creaked open to reveal a surprisingly untangled front yard and a well-trodden concrete path that lit up beneath their feet. The sight was pure relief to Poppy, who had started to worry that maybe vegetation had completely consumed the cottage and she'd have to hack her way into it.

Someone had obviously mowed it recently. Even the edges along the path had been trimmed. Poppy gave a jump of excitement. Although it obviously needed some TLC, before her stood the cutest little blue-grey weatherboard cottage she had ever seen. It looked like it belonged on the pages of a Country Style magazine. A tiny porch greeted her and framed a beautiful old timber door. And, although its white paint chipped off in every direction, it held snug the most gorgeous pink and green glass lead light window, complete with an Art déco style tulip pattern. "It's *amazing*. And look at all the yard space."

Poppy was so captivated she had almost forgotten about Nica, who shivered next to her. "I don't mean to be a downer but I'm pretty sure my toes have frost bite. Do you think we could find that key?"

"Sorry, sure thing. I've just got to find the letterbox." Poppy shone her torch light back toward the front gate. "Ah, huh!"

All but hidden underneath a rather large passion

fruit vine was an old tin mailbox ready to fall off the fence. It screeched in protest as Poppy forced its lid open. Bits of rusty nail fell out from under it. Inside was an envelope with Poppy's name written on it. "Here it is." It jingled as she picked it up. "I can take it from here. Thanks a bunch for dropping me off. You're a lifesaver."

"I'm not going to leave until you've opened the door. What if it's the wrong key?" said Nica, jiggling on the spot—her hands buried in her armpits, for warmth.

Poppy could tell Nica was more than happy to stay by the genuine concern in her voice but there was a part of her that wanted to step foot inside her new home on her own. "It won't be. It's got my name on the envelope. I'll be fine, seriously. You've done more than enough and you must be ready to call it a night."

"Are you sure? I really don't mind," yawned Nica, still jiggling.

"Absolutely. Don't worry about me, I'm a city girl." Poppy watched Nica hold back another yawn. She was grateful for her new friend. "I wish I could offer you a cup of tea but I'm not sure how well stocked the pantry is or even if there's a kettle."

"No worries at all. Let's take a rain check. And hey, you won't be a city girl for long. I reckon you'll be hanging up your high heels for gumboots in not time," Nica laughed—her nose ring sparkling in the torchlight.

"I recon you might be right." Poppy, who was

overcome with the feeling of being in the right place at the right time, couldn't wait to be sloshing around her new backyard, pruning this and planting that. This is where she belonged. All the vision boards, all the manifestation meditations and prayers had finally paid off.

Nica turned and waved a friendly goodbye. "I'll see you soon."

"Sure will," Poppy nodded as she waved back. She waited until Nica had shut the car door before dragging her suitcase to the front porch of Page Cottage. The light from her mobile illuminated the keyhole. A squeal escaped as she happy danced for just a second, relishing in the moment of achievement. The anticipation of her perfect country abode was more than Poppy could bear. So what if the garden desperately needed a style cut? She could take care of that later, and who knows? In the sunlight, it really might not be so bad.

CHAPTER 5

Poppy flicked the light switch on the inside of the door up and down. Nothing. "What the heck?" she tried again. Nothing. Her stomach dropped. She was getting the feeling that maybe she had missed an integral email about electricity at the property—or the lack of it, to be correct. Her mobile torch flashed light into the room and revealed a quaint tongue and grove-clad lounge, painted the same antique blue colour as the train station. There was a rose patterned lounge suite, a yellow crocheted rug, pot-bellied stove in the far corner and wooden floorboards that creaked as she crossed them in search of another light switch to test. *Flick. Flick.* Nothing. Still nothing.

"Crap!"

Although it was strangely quiet compared to the city, the house moaned and somewhere outside, an owl hooted. A cool draft blew in from a crack in one of the double-hung windows. Next to the stove were split logs neatly arranged in a stack according to their different sizes. It brought Poppy a world of joy to also find some firelighters, kindling, a box of matches and, surprisingly, a kettle in a tin bucket behind one of the old lounges. She had never built a fire before, but considered tonight as perfect a time as any to learn. Plus, she wasn't sure how she was going to survive the night with no heating. It was only mildly warmer inside than out.

The rest of the house revealed a narrow hall with two small bedrooms, one with a four-poster wrought iron bed and the other with a single bed that looked like it had never been used. There was also an old laminate bathroom and a yellow Formica kitchen that must have been very fancy in its day but now smelt sour and musty —rather like an old damp library that had been locked away for years. This didn't concern Poppy. What did was the absence of a loo. The cottage wasn't that big, Poppy had counted ten paces from one end to the other. She guessed the laundry might be in the garage but surely there was a toilet? Poppy walked through the darkness down the hall once again counting the rooms. Nope. No toilet. She felt the blood drain from her face. *Oh no. It can't be.* She had read about them, seen pictures even, little tin shacks in the backyard. But surely not *here*. Surely not in a house that was meant for her to live in for three entire months?

Poppy pushed open a wooden door at the end of the hall and shone her trusty mobile torch light down a small set of steps and into the back yard. Amongst a failing chicken coop, rusty potting shed and old greenhouse, stood something looking suspiciously like one of her worst nightmares. An outhouse.

Poppy cursed. Why did she need to pee now? Stepping out, she began what seemed like a treacherous journey. Following a rather narrow dirt path, her heart skipped a beat with every rustle and flutter. She wished Nica were still here. This was not the dreamlike moment she'd imagined her first night, in her perfect country cottage, to be. She wondered if it would not be best just to hoist up her skirt and be done with it right next to what she could now see was a raised garden bed home to a diverse and towering collection of weeds. *Surely no one will see.* Poppy leant her phone against a tuft of grass and squatted into position. She couldn't remember the last time she'd whizzed in the open air. It was quite liberating. As she did, her mind skipped from how frosty the air felt on her bare skin to how best to light a fire. A square stack would do, she decided, having seen it done in books about Scandinavian wood stacking. It looked simple enough. *Gaby's probably stacking 'Bloody Bastard's' wood right now.*

Poppy stood and pulled up her underwear. Picking up her phone she relished in her resilience. Not only had she peed outdoors she'd also remembered how to light a fire and was now looking forward to a hot cup of tea and a shower. She knew she couldn't use the backyard path as her bathroom forever but right now she felt like some sort of capable super woman who could handle anything.

For a second, Poppy stood with her eyes closed and soaked in the night. The air smelt cold and fresh. The landscape was quiet. As she opened her eyes to the sky, an eternity of stars sparkled above. It was one of those awe-inspiring moments that remind you, life is beautiful. If it had not been for the almighty bang and cacophony of hisses that sent her jumping a mile high, she could have remained lost in it for hours.

What the bloody hell was that?

Poppy turned on her heals and sprinted. No longer did she feel she could tackle beasts. In fact, she felt like the first thing she would have to do when she got back inside was open her suitcase and find a clean pair of underwear. With the door firmly shut behind her, she took a moment to gather her breath. She had never moved so fast. She wasn't sure what had been so ready to unceremoniously maul her to death in her new backyard but she sure as hell wasn't going back out there to find out.

CHAPTER 6

Poppy stared blankly at the flames as they glowed warmth into the tiny lounge. She was chuffed with herself for mastering fire so quickly and felt a satisfaction that early man must have also enjoyed as they huddled in their caves, gnawing on the delicious hind leg of wooly mammoth. Poppy was pleased that the self-sufficiency books she'd been devouring for the last few years were finally paying off. First, she placed two larger logs at the outer edges of the firebox, before arranging the kindling and firelighters in the middle. Then she carefully stacked the split timber from smallest to largest in a neat and towering grid formation, allowing room for airflow. She crossed her fingers as she struck a match and threw it toward the firelighters. After a few deep breaths and a couple of powerful blows into the belly of the stove, the kindling had caught alight, and the flames started to lick the timbers. It wasn't long before the fire roared to life and heat filled the room.

Poppy's body thawed and her shoulders melted into the couch with every sip from her cup of tea. She had felt blessed by magical tea fairies upon discovering that the stove in the kitchen was gas, that water did indeed trickle out of the pipes, albeit with much coughing and spluttering, and that a tin of loose leaf earl grey had been left in the cupboard, all of which helped her forget about the small animal droppings that were also littered in there. The mug she found sported a Gryffindor crest, so, all in all the night had turned out quite enjoyable.

Poppy wondered how she had been so unprepared. How did she not know that she needed to hook electricity up to the house? It was then that she saw a white envelope propped up on the side table next to the front door.

Dear Miss MacLuster,

Welcome to Derrin! By now you would have received the instructions for your accommodation, Page Cottage.

You will of course know that you needed to make your own arrangements to have electricity connected to the property, so as to have power upon arrival. The hot water system, stove and oven are all gas and you should have enough supply to last you the next three months. However, the pump that pumps water from the tank to the house requires electricity, so in order to have water, you will first need to have electricity. Without power to the pump, you will get little more than a cup of water from the pipes before they run dry.

As you would have by now seen, the property is moderately furnished to meet your basic needs with comfort. Unfortunately, the previous tenant suffered illness and as a consequence the gardens are quite run down. You mentioned in your letter of expression of interest that you look forward to the outdoor life so we feel you would be suited to give the property the attention that is needed. Page Cottage is a special place and we are sure you will enjoy living here. Please do not make any changes to the building without written permission.

As suggested in the letter of appointment, we recommend you change your mobile phone reception and internet provider to Telstra, or a company that uses Telstra's network, if you haven't already, as no other companies will offer you service this far out of the city.

To reiterate previous communication, the outhouse replacement has been delayed due to Council funding being committed elsewhere. The key to the courtesy vehicle, provided to you during your position, is in the cutlery draw in the kitchen. We remind you that the vehicle runs on diesel.

Please ensure you collect your key to the library, when you arrive in Derrin. As outlined in my email to you, two days ago, you will be expected to open the library at 9:00 am on Tuesday 2nd July. You will close the library at 4:00 pm each day.

Any questions, please do not hesitate to contact me.

Kind regards,

Ms. Shirley Baxter

Human Resources Manager

Human Resources Department

Derrin Shire Council

Crap! Keys? Electricity? Poppy found it hard to be excited about the courtesy car when she was drowning in a sinking feeling that screamed, "YOU'VE MISSED A WHOLE HEAP OF EMAILS." How they never made it to her inbox, Poppy would never know and as someone who liked to be prepared, the thought of a stressful start to her first day, made her uneasy. What else was she missing? And how was she going to iron her clothes? Anxiety crept in. There was nothing she could do about it now. She'd just have to hope that come morning, if she got to the library early enough, someone would be able to show her where the key was. That was, if anyone was around who knew.

CHAPTER 7

Morning was breaking over the horizon when Poppy awoke to a chorus of birdsong. Magpies called out in celebration of a new day and Poppy found it humorous to watch them hop about gathering their breakfast. She was delighted to find that the backyard was not nearly as overgrown as the dark of night had made her believe. In fact, though it needed work, there was a certain charm to its rambling sprawl that Poppy found quite pleasant. What Poppy hadn't expected to see when she popped her head out the kitchen window, that morning, was a house not ten meters from her own. Their lawn, whose ever it was, was immaculate and the gardens would have given Versailles a run for its money. On the other side of what was definitely a rambling mess in comparison, were perfectly pruned rose bushes, an array of herbs, neatly trellised vegetables, trimmed citrus and even a few topiary. Poppy wondered who her mysterious neighbour was and whether it was they she had to thank for the mowed lawn.

It had been almost midnight when Poppy had fallen asleep on the couch curled up in front of the fire, snug in a blanket she had found in one of the bedroom wardrobes. She'd dreamt of vine tendrils slithering like snakes into the cottage and wrapping themselves around the walls. As a result, Poppy woke with a vow to tame the yard as quickly as possible, and looking out across her neighbour's personal Eden only affirmed her resolve.

Poppy grabbed the car keys from the cutlery draw and readied herself for her first day as Derrin's trusted librarian. She wondered what her staff would be like and who her customers were. The only things that were missing from her morning were her having a set of keys to the actual library and a freshly ironed outfit. Flattening the pleats on her skirt as best she could, Poppy grabbed her glasses and made her way out the front door over to the garage. She'd never been provided a car before and the excitement was making her feel giggly. *Wait until Rachel hears about this,* she mused as she pushed the large old iron door open.

Poppy gulped. The 'vehicle' was not just a vehicle. It was a monster truck. Poppy had only ever seen cars this gigantic on television. She wondered whatever possessed Derrin Council to think that a ute was suitable librarian transport. She was only tiny. Poppy wasn't even sure she could get in the thing let alone be confident her feet would reach the pedals or that she would be able to see over the steering wheel. *Please don't let it be manual. Please don't let it be manual.* She hadn't driven a manual before but Sven had learnt to drive in one and he'd told many a horror story of how 'The Beast' as it was known, kept popping out of gear and stalling. Poppy was terrified. She ran inside and grabbed a cushion, just in case she needed a booster seat. *No one needs to know*, she told herself.

Farmland stretched out as far as the eye could see. Emerald drops of dew clung to the Kikuyu grass and glistened in the morning light. Anticipation tingled in Poppy's stomach. Eagerness for her first day bubbled inside her. This was the opportunity she'd been waiting for her entire career and finally her dreams were coming true. She didn't care one iota that she didn't yet have a way of getting into the library, that she had to have a bird bath in the kitchen sink, that breakfast comprised of dandelion leaves plucked from the edges of the old chicken coop, she'd learnt to recognise their single flowering stems and soft leaves from studying a weed forager's guide, or that her morning meditation had been interrupted by a horrible screechy cry that had just about given her an out of body experience. None of these things, Poppy gave a damn about. Because, right now, she was cruising into town in her very own pickup truck —one that started and one without a column shift. Everything seemed perfect. That was until Poppy hit her very own pothole and not the bitumen kind.

She didn't know where the library was.

And she couldn't Google it.

Poppy sat in the truck's cabin rubbing her lotus tattoo and trying to think rationally. *Okay, Derrin is about the size of a postage stamp. Surely it can't take too long to find the damn place. I mean if I were a library where would I be? Near a park? Council building?* Poppy remembered her offer of employment letter had mentioned that the library was one of a collection of buildings with a garden — which Nica mentioned as being overgrown. What it was with her attracting disheveled gardens into her life, Poppy didn't know. Maybe it was some sort of metaphor for her taming her own desires and growing into the person she'd always felt herself to be. Maybe it was purely that there weren't the funds to put toward maintaining such thing as a community garden, although Poppy thought it essential. She had never truly had a garden herself, just a few plants in pots. One of which was a misunderstood, yet quite friendly when you got to know it, Bunya pine. Its leaves were so spikey her friends had called him 'Dodgy Prick'. Poppy thought it rather a cruel name for a plant that was just being itself.

She missed her friends although she had lost touch with many of them, most being married and with children. Her being the only one who didn't have a husband or little ones, she found herself slowly being excluded from family friendly invites. Why her friends didn't think she would enjoy outings to places like Bouncing World was beyond Poppy. Bouncing was the best and she could still do it without peeing her pants, a gift, that now escaped many of her girlfriends whose vaginas had been stretched by baby heads. Of course, she had Sven and Carl, her sister, and now Nica, but Poppy was super excited to meet new people and become a part of her new hometown. That's if she didn't get fired for not turning up on her first day.

Poppy wasn't sure where to begin her search. It was 7:00 am and probably way too early for any Council staff to be working. She also wasn't exactly sure how big Derrin was, but it was smaller than Sydney so that was a positive. She sat parked outside a quaint café surveying her surroundings and looking for clues like Agatha Raisin. Derrin had one main street and two not so main streets that ran parallel to each other. The main street had the pub. That's how Poppy knew it was the main street. Plus, it was called Main Street. The street to the left was called Derrin Road and the one to the right was called Cock Ball Street. Poppy vowed to find out why. None of them had a signpost for the library. This would have been worrying if it were not for the miracle that was Nica.

"Mornin' sunshine!" a very awake Nica banged on the driver's side window, almost scaring a pre-coffee bowel movement out of Poppy. Dressed in a bright yellow trench coat and matching headscarf that tamed her unruly red ringlets, Poppy thought she looked the vision of a sunflower. "How'd you sleep last night?" Nica beamed, as she took a sip from her reusable pottery take-away cup. Poppy made a mental note to get one. This town was far more hipster than she had first expected. In her short time counting streets, Poppy had also counted thirteen cafes. *Thirteen.*

"Oh boy, am I glad to see you." Poppy was truly grateful to see Nica's face. "You don't by any chance know where the key to the library is do you?"

"You can stop looking so terrified. I have it," Nica giggled. Poppy took a sigh of relief as Nica pulled a key that looked like it could open a castle door out of her pocket. "Carmel had a feeling that you may not have been getting her, or Shirley Baxter's, emails."

"I haven't. I had no idea that I needed a key. I hadn't received any instruction and assumed someone from Council would be there to meet me on my first day and that there'd be a security code for an alarm system or something."

Nica laughed and shook her head. "Oh honey, there

ain't no security system and I'm your welcoming party. Come on. I'll show you how to get there."

Nica skipped around to the passenger side of the truck, popped the door open and jumped up into the seat like she'd done the manoeuvre a million times. "It's just a minute down Cock Ball Street—nice booster seat!" she chuckled, balancing her takeaway mug between her knees and clicking in the seatbelt.

"Yeah, unfortunately these old trucks aren't made for the vertically challenged," Poppy laughed. "I'm grateful my feet reach the pedals." Once all was clear, she crunched the gear stick into first and set off down the road. The seat they sat on bounced up and down and Poppy thought if she closed her eyes they could be in some bumpy wagon in colonial times; dressed in big skirts and whale bone corsets, off to buy ham hocks or have tea with the local millinery. After a lifetime of city living, Derrin seemed old-fashioned in a very trendy way. The buildings had kept their country charm. Some shop fronts presented wooden bay windows, little verandahs and window boxes. They sold things such as handmade chocolates, organic hemp clothing, local artisan crafts, boutique vegan products and antiques. Poppy felt much more at ease now that she was no longer worried about getting into the library. She listened to Nica chat about the town's history.

"Derrin was founded by settlers looking to farm dairy cattle. Once the land was deemed viable, other families moved here wanting to get away from Sydney's slums. The shops in this street cater to tourists but over in Derrin Road you have your farm co-op, work-wear shop, doctors and the like. Main Street has the pub, cafes, restaurants and some more shops that the hipsters orgasm over."

Poppy chuckled.

"It's true. I've seen them. This town is nuts on the weekend," grinned Nica.

"So what's with the name Cock Ball Street then?"

Nica giggled and Poppy wondered if there was ever a time that she didn't. "Cock Ball Street. Legend has it, that in 1920, the Mayor of Derrin was witnessing a game of shuttlecock between two cattlemen. There was a bet that if one of the cattlemen could hit the street sign —which was North Street back then—the Mayor would name the street after the first thing he saw. Well, one of the balls went rogue after a big hit and hit the street sign and the first thing the Mayor saw was a bullock train crossing the road and a bull that he reckoned had the biggest cock and balls he'd ever seen. The Mayor being a man of his word aptly named the street Cock Ball Street."

Poppy couldn't stop laughing. "*That is* bull. No way is that true."

"I swear it is! Well, most of it," Nica winked. "I'm a bit sketchy on the year. Okay, slow down. We are coming up to the driveway."

Poppy's jaw dropped. A jungle had begun to emerge from the end of the street. "It is actually worse than I thought."

"It's pretty bad. Carmel, who you know was the previous manager, took a lot of sick leave and the place sort of got forgotten about. Library volunteers have run it for the last few months. Things will need a lot of looking at that's for sure."

"I never knew weeds could grow so high and the cottage's back yard is full of them."

Nica gave a carefree shrug. "There is a bit of pruning to do. But now that you're here you'll be able to sort it out and have this place looking spiffy in no time."

Daunted by the task in front of her, Poppy nodded. "In no time," she repeated trying her hardest to sound optimistic.

"Oh and the library's book collection will probably need looking at. The volunteers have done their best, but they struggled to throw anything away based on prosperity. There are some items in there I wouldn't take to bed that's for sure. So, speaking of balls, do you have a man back in Sydney?" Nica asked catching Poppy off-guard. "I mean, I guess I shouldn't assume but you don't seem like someone who identifies as part of the LBGTQIA community."

Poppy almost stalled the truck. "Um, no, I'm not. And no, I don't have a man back home. I had a geriatric male cat, if that counts, he died last year, but no. No man. Not for a while actually. My last boyfriend was a narcissistic arse and immature drunk who ran off with a cocktail guzzling backpacker. I've been a bit gun shy ever since. Plus, I worked such long hours in Sydney so I didn't really go out much."

Nica raised her eyebrows. It was as if she couldn't believe what she was hearing. "How long ago was this?"

"About five years," coughed Poppy.

Nica squeaked. "Five years! But you're gorgeous. Look at you. Petite, long brown hair, size nothing, cute pink glasses. Kind, funny—I'm not hitting on you I swear—I just can't believe that you haven't dated anyone or had sex for *five* years."

"The time doesn't go quickly, believe me."

"Maybe you'll meet a nice country boy here. Someone to take home to mama."

"Mama is overseas yachting around the Caribbean with Papa. It would be nice to meet someone, though. Someone kind and warm-hearted, and not a drunk."

"Universe! Please bring Poppy a forever love who is kind, warm hearted and damn sexy." Nica's eyes sparkled. "Hey what about that guy at the bar, last night? I saw him look over at you a couple of times."

"What guy? Wait do you mean Mr. Grumpy?"

Nica nodded.

Although it was barely ten degrees outside, Poppy wished the truck had air conditioning. "He is *not* interested in me at all. I think he made that pretty clear. He was probably just looking at me to make sure he knew where I was, so he could avoid running into me. That's all."

"How do you know that? He doesn't even know you."

"He was rude to me not once but twice." Poppy could tell that she was blushing. Nica didn't have to know that the vision of his tanned forearms and sexy lips had haunted her since last night. Which Poppy thought ridiculous considering the man's attitude was abhorrent.

"Who knows, you might run into him again pretty soon," Nica grinned.

After driving through a wire mesh gate, the type that Poppy thought could be found bordering an old schoolyard or detention centre, she and Nica pulled up in the staff car park behind the library. Poppy's heart fluttered as they walked around to the front of the building. It was beautiful. Run down, yes, but beautiful. The place had so much potential, and she wondered again why it had fallen into such neglect, Poppy listened to Nica give a brief summary of what was before them.

The library was the main building, a post-war timber cottage, clad in heritage red panels and white trim. It had a small landing that currently provided shelter for a family of swallow's and their nest. The building, which used to be the local bank, had been shifted there fifty years ago, when the mobile library service became too expensive for Derrin Shire Council to maintain. The shed-like structure to the left of the library was now the art studio where Nica ran her art classes. And on the other side of the garden, just visible through the towering cobblers pegs and nasturtiums, was an old worker's cottage, which had been turned into the Men's Shed. Poppy decided that one of the first things she would do in her new role, would be to mow. Or rather, find someone who could.

She waited as Nica used the key that looked like a medieval relic to unlock the front door of the library. Inside revealed that two of the building's walls had been removed to create an open space for the collections and a check out area at the entrance. A smaller room remained and held the library's two public computers.

"And where do I make a cup of tea?" asked Poppy, feeling a bit overwhelmed.

Nica pointed to the back of the library. "There's a kettle and bathroom down there. The volunteers may have left some tea but I wouldn't touch the milk. Gladys, who's in charge, doesn't have a good sense of smell. I saw some bread in the freezer and Vegemite in the cupboard though, if you need a snack."

"What else do the volunteers do around here?" Poppy asked as they walked to the back of the library toward the tearoom.

"This and that. Shelve things, I think. Raise money

—although that hasn't happened for a while..." Nica paused. "Actually, apart from shelve books, drink tea and arrange the cut flowers, which obviously hasn't happened for a while either," Nica nodded toward a mouldy, dried bunch of flowers sitting stagnant in a vase on the kitchenette bench, "I'm not sure what they do."

"And when do the other staff turn up?"

"The others?" Nica shook her head. "There aren't any others. It's just you."

"What?" Surely she'd heard incorrectly. "It's. Just. Me?" gulped Poppy.

"Yep. Just you, and the volunteers, or 'vollies' as I like to call them. But don't worry. There's a manual for everything under the desk. Carmel was very organised. She also struggled to step into the twenty-first century so there's a paper record for every process. She used the computer to issue the collection items though so don't worry about that. It's not a full date stamp situation."

"Well, that's a relief. Geez, now I really need a cup of tea."

"Seriously, don't worry about anything. Gladys will probably be in today and if anything's not making sense, she'll be able to show you. I'm pretty sure Gladys was hoping she'd be in charge until Carmel came back from sick leave, though. So, be warned, she's a bit miffed about not running the joint. It might take her a couple of days to warm to you. The vollies are a political bunch that's for sure. Lots of alpha CWA type females, if you get my meaning."

"Country Women's Association?"

"Yep. Great ladies but you wouldn't want to cross 'em in a dark alley holding a rolling pin," Nica answered cheekily.

"Right well, I'll be sure to be nice as winning pie then." Poppy's stomach churned slightly. She rubbed her lotus tattoo.

"They'll love you. They'll probably try to set you up with their grandsons," Nica reassured.

"Oh gosh. I had neighbours like that, back in Sydney. Always trying to set me up. It never worked." A brief memory of the time when Sven and Carl had tried to set her up with a gym junkie flashed into Poppy's mind. As it turned out the man had an undisclosed breast milk addiction, true story, and she thought being asked on the first date if she'd ever lactated was a step too far. Poppy wondered how Sven was going finding a sublet and made a mental note to email he and Carl later.

"I get the feeling we could natter on all day. But I've got to get crackin' and set up for today's pottery class. It's coil pots and I'm expecting a full class from the local respite centre." Nica's eyes smiled. That is what someone who's high on life looks like, Poppy mused.

Poppy closed the door behind Nica and locked it again. She needed time to settle into the space without interruption. She also needed to find the procedures that Carmel had left her because without them it was going to be a long day. But first tea. Poppy couldn't start the day without a potent brew. It was better than breakfast and always worked wonders to calm her nerves. And today, she was feeling quite under prepared. Having no staff and volunteers that already had their noses out of joint wasn't going to make for an easy first day but Poppy reminded herself that back in Sydney the customers loved her, especially the senior ones. She had a way of connecting with people, listening to them and making them feel seen. If she could do it in Sydney, she could do it here. *What's the worst that could happen?* She cheered herself on.

Poppy was revealing in the serenity when a loud bang at the entrance door caused her to jump and spill her earl grey on the hardwood timber floor. *Surely it's not opening time already?* Rushing to get a cloth from the kitchenette, Poppy caught site of a minibus load of young adults, through one of the library's windows. She assumed they were from a local respite centre as wheelchairs and scooters slowly disembarked into the hub's car park, while the rest of the group stood patiently with their carers.

BANG. BANG. BANG.

"Coming," called Poppy, feelings of dread

descending. She could hear Nica's upbeat voice welcoming her morning's art class.

Poppy pulled her mobile phone out of her pocket to check how close the time was to opening. She pressed the buttons hoping it would wake up but there were no signs of life. It was completely dead.

BANG. BANG. BANG.

"Coming!" Poppy called again, forgetting her search for something to clean the floor with. She hoped the racket wasn't one of the volunteers come to check up on her. With the remaining tea in hand, she dashed from the back of the library toward the entrance, completely disregarding the puddle on the floor. That was until she slipped and went bottom up, her head narrowly missing the front counter.

"Everything alright in there?" a commanding voice boomed from the other side of the entrance door.

"Sorry!" Poppy scrambled to her feet, her carefully curated outfit now sporting light brown wet patches. Patting down her frazzled self, she tried her best to embody the calmness of someone who had things under control and a perfectly good excuse for being late. It didn't work. Because on the other side of the door was Aiden Baxter.

CHAPTER 8

"It's you!" Poppy felt heat tingle her skin and her breath quickened. The tall, dark-haired and handsome, bicep flexing, flannelette wearing country boy, who had eye-rolled her hot pink pumps, stood before her.

"It's me," he replied without emotion. "Aiden Baxter." Aiden pointed to the badge pinned to his Paris-blue uniform. "Senior Firefighter. You have a Maintenance Inspection Report booked for this morning. Is everything alright in here?"

"Yes. Yes! All right. Yes," Poppy could have died. She sounded idiotic and just short of an orgasm. "Sorry. I'm Poppy. Poppy MacLuster." Poppy reached out and shook Aiden's hand. It was warm, soft and rough in patches. She could tell he was no stranger to hard work.

"I heard a loud bang and then someone say 'what

the dickens!'" the corner of Aiden's lips lifted revealing dimples in his cheeks. "Was that you?" he smirked.

"Yes. And I'm okay," replied Poppy haughtily, pushing her glasses up her nose and trying not to draw attention to the tea stains on her blouse and skirt. "Would you mind giving me a minute? I'm sure you can get started without me." Poppy all but ran out the back. She wanted a sinkhole to open up and swallow her. She listened as Aiden Baxter, the dead set sexiest man she'd ever seen outside of Netflix, rhythmically made his way around the library—stopping every so often to mutter a 'hmm' or 'that'll need looking at', before starting again.

"Is everything okay?" Poppy called out from the backroom. She practically had to soak the front of her outfit to remove the tea stains.

When she did finally emerge, Aiden was up a ladder. A pile of brown soaked tissues formed a soggy pile on one of the rungs.

"Thanks for mopping up the mess," she replied gratefully.

Aiden, who concentrated on his task, reached his brawny arms up to the ceiling. "No worries. Couldn't have you slipping again."

Poppy watched the way his shoulders flexed and his tanned hands delicately replaced the case on one of the fire alarms. He made a note on his clipboard.

"Is everything okay?" she repeated.

Poppy watched the way his brows farrowed. He said

nothing. She stepped forward trying to get a closer look at what was such a concern, unknowing that at the same time, Aiden would step down from the ladder. Which would have been fine. But by now, Poppy was so close that his crotch practically landed in her face. Her glasses tumbled to the ground.

"Hey, watch out!" Aiden, wide eyed and clearly in shock, looked violated.

"I am so sorry!" Poppy felt mortified. Crouching to the ground she grappled for her specs. *I cannot believe I have just nosed his willy.* She could have died. Again. It was the closest she'd been to a man in five years and all she could think of was hiding.

Aiden, who was clearly a normal human and in charge of his senses, took a deep breath and adjusted his belt. He bent down and handed Poppy her glasses before returning to clipboard. She slid them back onto her nose. Feeling like an embarrassed naughty schoolgirl, she stood rubbing her tattoo and waiting for that sinkhole.

"There is a lot to do here." Aiden took his pen and started pointing it toward the different parts in the library. "Basically, the building doesn't meet the fire and safety standards. The fire alarms need replacing with ones that are wired into the power. The evacuation plans aren't placed correctly in the building and the equipment missed its last inspection. I'll need to check the other structures on the way out but I'm pretty certain they are all going to be the same. Is the staff and volunteer training up to date?"

Poppy's eyes must have glazed over because Aiden tutted and continued to make notes.

"Sorry but this is my first day. I didn't even know you were going to be here."

"You should have been told. These checks happen routinely," Aiden replied matter-of-factly. "Carmel said she put it in the calendar and an email."

"I haven't started up the computer yet. And I haven't read my email or the calendar." *Bloody emails.* Poppy couldn't believe how much information she'd missed.

"Well, I advise you do. I'm guessing there's a lot in there you'll need to read. This place is in pretty bad shape but luckily not as bad as the last report indicated. Structurally, it's okay. Usually, I'm the one to do the inspections but I was on leave when the last report was due and my colleague Mattie took care of it. I'll need to book in another inspection in two weeks time. You'll have to ensure that you're on your way to bringing the building to compliance, by then." Aiden ripped a duplicate copy of the report he'd just completed from his clipboard and handed it to Poppy. As he did, his brown eyes landed fleetingly on her damp blouse. Poppy wondered why he was blushing. She looked across the room and caught sight of her reflection in the window.

Holy heck!

Poppy had no idea she had been giving Aiden a wet shirt show. Snapping her arms across her now very visible nipples, she wanted to kick herself for deciding not to wear a bra that morning. *It is safe to assume,* she thought, *today is not going well.*

It had taken Aiden another thirty-five silent minutes to complete his inspection of the rest of the community hub. Poppy had stayed in the library unable to shake the nippily tea-stained horror of her morning. When he had emerged, still unable to meet her eye, it was with not-so-great news. The community hub was indeed not up to fire and safety standards. And it would have to be. Poppy knew she would have to check her emails. There had to be some major information that she was missing. She still didn't understand why the premises were so unkempt. Especially considering they appeared to have such potential as a vibrant community space. Poppy was lost in deep thought when she heard another bang on the door.

"What's going on?! Why aren't you open?" someone called out gruffly.

Open? Poppy froze. *OH NO.* Poppy scrambled to the door hoping with all hope that it wasn't Aiden again. It wasn't.

An elderly man stood before her, hunched over with

white-knuckled and gnarled fingers clenched to a stack of books. A motorised scooter, which Poppy assumed was his, blocked off the entrance to the library like he owned the place. His weathered brows farrowed causing his wispy white eyebrows to join into one disharmonious monobrow situation, making him look like the apple Poppy had dried as part of her preschool project to recreate her granny. Her granny had been just about as impressed as this man was now.

Pushing past Poppy, he stood at the front counter dinging the bell. "I'd like to speak to someone who works here. Where's Gladys?"

"Um, I'm the one who works here. Gladys isn't here. I'm Poppy MacLuster, the new Librarian."

The man's wrinkles screwed into an angry ball. "MacLuster, hey. That'd be right. Send an unqualified junior out to the regional library, we won't know any better."

"I'm sorry, what was your name sir?" asked Poppy, flabbergasted by the attitude being thrown her way.

"Mr. Jenkins. I've been coming to the library since it was a bookshelf in the Council building. Then it was a mobile library, you probably don't know that. Now, I come here. The service is *usually* great."

Poppy had been grateful for Nica's lowdown, although, why she hadn't mentioned Mr. Jenkins seemed an oversight. "I know that it used to be a mobile library, Mr. Jenkins, but thank you for sharing with me that the library started as a shelf in the Council Chambers. I didn't know that. You must be very knowledgeable about the area." The paltry attempt to flatter Mr. Jenkins seemed to work. He dumped his books on the counter and began a rather lengthy spiel about the history of the library according to who had been in charge and how amazing a job they had done, Carmel, apparently was unsurpassed. Poppy tried her best to be interested but secretly wished Mr. Jenkins would bugger off so she could get onto figuring out how to run the library. She could see the several tomes left behind by Carmel, the wonder librarian, and was both eager and dreading reading them.

It was fifteen minutes later that Mr. Jenkins left in a huff over not being able to find the western he wanted in large print. Usually, Poppy felt uneasy about a customer leaving unsatisfied but this time she was quite happy to see the back of Mr. Jenkins and his motorised scooter. Secretly, she hoped to not get any customers for the rest of the morning at least not until she'd figured out how to issue items to borrowers and had also figured out how items were returned. Given that Mr. Jenkins had demanded the books he had borrowed be returned from his library account as a matter of urgency, she thought it best to get the basics sorted as soon as possible. Feeling energetically drained and still mortified, she wondered if anyone other than Mr. Jenkins would notice if she closed the library for the day? Wishing it were possible, Poppy picked up the procedure manual labeled 'Number 1' and switched on the front desk computer. At least she could do that much. Thankfully, inside the folder was a detailed instruction on how to open the library. And although she was now an hour late in doing so, Poppy got started straight away.

With the lack of fancy digital technology, it took Poppy just under fifteen minutes to turn on the public computers, straighten the shelves, and locate the returns chute hidden behind the magazine shelving. Poppy thought it a miracle that the software and cataloguing systems used by Derrin Public Library were the same ones she'd used in the city. The discovery almost brought tears of gratitude to her eyes.

With the library finally ready for customers, Poppy got down to opening her email. She'd deal with her inbox in a moment but first she wanted to compose an email to Sven.

Hi ho, neighbour! How's it going over in the big smoke?

Just wanted to check in and see how the sublet's going on my flat. Email seems pretty ancient but my phone doesn't have any reception at the moment. Will text when I get some. My start to Derrin has been interesting. Yesterday I peed outside in the wilderness that is my backyard and today I had a sexy fireman's

crotch in my face. No need to ask any questions. Love
Pops x

With sent clicked Poppy opened her Inbox and
began to read her emails.

"Hiya!" it was almost lunchtime when a sunny Nica
skipped into the library. "How's your morning going?"

"Horrific." Poppy slumped into the chair behind the
front counter. "I officially met Aiden, nosed his privates,
flashed my nipples and found out that the entire
community hub is at risk of combusting at any moment.
I've only had one customer, which is a good thing
because I've only just had time to read the procedure
manuals. Oh, and you were right. There are lots of
books on the shelves that should be put in the bin."
Poppy rattled off the morning's adventures so fast that
Nica was left standing with her eyebrows raised in
disbelief.

"I'm sorry, go back to that bit about nosing privates
and exposing your boobs?" she said rather confused.

Poppy dropped her head into her hands. "Oh Nica, it
was awful! I was such an idiot. I bet he never wants to
see me again."

"What happened?"

"Long story, short, the guy from the pub, Aiden,

came to do the fire maintenance inspection or whatever it's called. Just before I heard his knock on the door, I slipped on tea that I'd spilt on the floor. I went arse over head and of course the rest of the tea went all over me. I opened the door in such a flap and realised he was the sexy but grumpy man from the pub. Went out the back to clean up. Had to wet my blouse to get the tea stain off but of course this place doesn't have a hand drier so found out too late that I couldn't dry it. But also didn't realise that my blouse was now see-through and, of course, I chose this morning not to wear a bra. I mean, I'm only an A cup, I can usually get away with it. Then like an idiot I came out and stood right under Aiden while he was on the ladder and when he climbed off it, my face was in prime position to nuzzle his bits. That's when I realised my nipples were 100% visible through my top."

"Wow." Nica's eyes were wide open and her mouth twitched. Poppy could tell she was lost for words. When she did speak, Poppy appreciated the effort she went to try to convince her that Aiden probably hadn't noticed.

"And who was your customer?" Nica asked, hesitantly. "Mr. Jenkins?" she grimaced.

"Yeah. He's a piece of work! I haven't had anyone else in though, which I'm a bit worried about."

"Ah don't be." Nica waved her hand lightly. "You won't get any customers this morning. It's free morning tea for senior citizens down at the community hall.

They'll be there solving the world's problems. Carmel always left the backroom tasks for a Tuesday morning knowing that the only customer she was likely to get was Mr. Jenkins. Who she swore only came in on a Tuesday so that he would get all her attention. She and I had an agreement that I would phone the library at 9:15 am pretending to need help. I tried calling this morning, but the phone went through to message bank. Haven't you read any of your emails yet? Carmel said she'd explained everything to get you through this morning."

Poppy let out a little insane chuckle. Her head fell into her hands. "Oh man, I could have done with your phone call this morning. I didn't even think to check if the phones were on a night mode. But what I've told you isn't even the bad bit. The thing is, I read my emails, after Mr. Jenkins left." Poppy took a deep breath.

"What? What could be worse?"

Poppy felt her face fall grave as she clicked open her emails again. "I've now got to find a way to bring the library and community hub grounds up to fire and safety compliance standards, with no budget because, for some reason, there's really only enough left in the budget to pay my wage. Listen to this:

Dear Miss MacLuster,

We wish to inform you that the library and community hub are in much need of maintenance.

Unfortunately, Council has had to withdraw much of its funding this year, due to competing priorities. One of your main tasks as the managing librarian will be to ensure the buildings and grounds are safety compliant by the end of your contracted period. If the buildings and grounds are not found to be safety complaint by the end of this period, it may force Council to withdraw funding all together and decommission the service.

Poppy closed the email.

"This is awful," said Nica, sounding devastated.

"I know. We have to raise money. And we have to do it fast.

Both girls sat in somber silence until Poppy felt herself perk up, with a spark of genius. "How many volunteers do we have here?"

Poppy listened as Nica listed the names of the people who volunteered regularly. "Well, there's Gladys, Jenny, and Claris for this place. Donald, Steve, Clive and Tony are over at the Men's Shed—I can introduce you to them tomorrow. And myself. Well, I earn a bit of money from my classes but if you count me, that makes eight."

"I think I may have a great idea."

"Ooh that sounds exciting," Nica grinned. "I love a great idea! Maybe I can cash in that cup of tea and we can both take a break? You can tell me all about it."

"Perfect!" Poppy placed the 'closed for lunch break' sign she'd found on the front porch and locked the entrance door. She led Nica to the back of the library and into the staff room. Waiting for the kettle to boil they both chatted easily.

"A fundraiser." Poppy knew it was a great idea. "We need to raise money to bring this place up to scratch and we don't have that long to do it. And we need to make the community garden into a place where people want to come and hang out. And we need to increase library membership. I ran a report in the library's borrower system and memberships have dropped by almost twenty percent in the last six months. That's heaps."

Nica nodded. Her eyes sparkled and Poppy could tell she was as excited by the idea as herself. "You're right Poppy, we can raise the funds we need ourselves and we can get the members back or new ones."

"We sure can. We just need to come up with some good ideas over the next week and then work out a plan of action. We're going to have to get sorted pretty much straight away, though. We don't have long and Aiden was pretty serious about the inspection not going well." Poppy took a sip from her teacup and unwrapped a Vegemite sandwich she'd made earlier with the stash that had been left in the library's kitchen. "How's your day going so far?" she asked, changing the subject.

Nica told Poppy all about her morning working with her additional needs students; how rewarding it was and how eager they were to have a go. She explained how art allowed them to express themselves in their own unique way and how everyone always had a success in an art class. "There are no wrongs in art class," beamed Nica. "Everything that is created is an artistic gem in its own right. I love it. The program runs until spring and we usually have an exhibition to celebrate. You'll have to come."

"I'd love to if I'm still here. My contract will be ending around then." Poppy felt her heart sadden. Three months was such a short time.

"You'll still be here. You're a country girl now, plus, you're going to meet the love of your life soon," stated Nica confidently.

"How do you know?" Poppy's eyes squinted. Nica looked sheepish.

"Okay. Okay. My tarot cards told me," said Nica as she took a sip from the steaming cup.

"Well after this morning's episode, I'm chuffed the cards think so," Poppy laughed, dismissing the idea.

"They do, they said that he's someone you've already met. Someone close by," smirked Nica over her teacup.

"Mr. Jenkins?" Both girls burst out laughing.

"What about you?" Poppy added. "You haven't told me if you have someone special in your life."

"I haven't? How odd," Nica toyed. "I've dated more men than you lately that's for sure."

"Oi!" Poppy pretended to be offended.

Nica shrugged. "I would like to meet someone but, honestly, I'm still getting over my last boyfriend. I was telling you about him on the drive out to your cottage. Things were going really great but then he broke it off because I didn't earn enough money, it really destroyed me."

"I still can't believe that was his reason." Poppy never had understood people who put money before love.

"I know but it's true," explained Nica. "I wasn't a big enough asset for him. He didn't see value in my art or anything. Thought I was a lovely person, but it wasn't enough. Of course, I deserve someone who isn't a shallow bastard. I just want to find someone who genuinely loves me, you know."

Poppy nodded. She knew all too well the desire to be loved unconditionally. Maybe, just maybe, Nica's tarot cards would turn out to be right. She might just find someone in the country who saw her for the kind and wonderful person she was. But first, she needed to find a way to save the community hub.

CHAPTER 9

Poppy was preparing to settle in for the afternoon, when a stout woman with tight blonde curls and a neatly pressed white skirt and top came bustling into the library, in an officiating whirlwind. She carried a tray of film wrapped oranges cut into quarters, like a woman whose sole job it was to hydrate the masses and stop the development of scurvy, and proclaimed something about a ludicrous bowl and how dare Trevor mention her oranges were tart. "They're bloody organic dear!"

"You must be the new lass? Here to replace Carmel? She was fabulous," the woman asked as she emerged from the staff room fridge, preening her curls back into shape.

"Yes. I am." Poppy watched as she totted around the kitchen wiping surfaces.

"I'm Gladys, dear. I was running this joint before

you were appointed but now I co-ordinate the volunteers. We each take turn in returning and shelving the books and setting up morning tea if there's an event. We also do a spot of gardening, but no one's been too keen on helping since Harold kicked the bucket over in the tomato patch."

Poppy who had taken a mouthful of water almost sprayed it over Gladys's neatly pressed bowling uniform. "I'm sorry, who died where?"

"Harold dear. A lovely and sometimes annoying man who ate and drank too much. He keeled over right amongst the Big Toms this January. Heart attack. Too much fraternising with the ladies down at the retirement village, if you ask me. Set his ticker off kilter. He's likely in purgatory." Gladys crossed herself like a devout Christian. "The rest of them reckon it's bad luck now. They all got scared. Haven't been able to get anyone to garden since then. Superstitious old fools."

Poppy liked Gladys's take no prisoner's attitude. It was intimidating but comical all the same and she was thinking she was going to enjoy having her around.

"I apologise for my abrupt entry but sometimes those old codgers really get up my goat." If they were anything like Mr. Jenkins, Poppy could understand why. "Looks like you've got everything in order in here?" nodded Gladys, approvingly.

"Yes, I think so. I'm just about to find someone who

has a whipper snipper to come in and tame the mess outside."

"Good luck to you dear," said Gladys, shaking her head. "I've tried every gardener in town. They all say they're busy. I even tried putting a flyer up at the high school to get a youngin' in. No luck. You might be able to charm someone in to do it though." Gladys offered with a raised eyebrow and shoulder shrug as if to say 'don't bother trying'. "Anyway, I've got books to return. I take it, you haven't done it?"

Poppy felt this was almost an accusation. Suddenly, she wasn't so sure whether Gladys and she would be great friends. "Um no. I haven't. The procedure mentioned that volunteers returned and shelved the books, so I was reluctant to start. I'm happy to do it though, especially when it's quiet. It'd be nice to have something to do that didn't require too much thinking."

"Too much thinking!" Gladys was outraged and Poppy knew as soon as the words had left her mouth that she'd put her foot in it. She winced as Gladys entered into a rant about brain flexibility, the Dewey system and returning being a very important job. "People would be up in arms if their books weren't returned off their cards! They'd get fines. It's a very detailed job that requires much concentration and our volunteers are very skilled at it, I'll have you know."

"Yes, of course. I didn't mean to suggest that your contribution wasn't important..."

"Contribution!"

Poppy had put her foot in it again. Gladys's face was like stone. Her lips pursed. Poppy was at a loss for words as to how this discussion had gotten so far out of hand. "I'll have you know," Gladys fumed, "we've single handedly kept this place open the last few months. We know just as much as you city folk about running a library."

"Gladys, I'm so sorry," Poppy started chanting the Ho'oponopono to herself, a Hawaiian prayer she'd learnt in meditation class for clearing up just about anything. *I'm sorry, forgive me.* "Really, I meant no offence. I really appreciate what you and the other volunteers have done, and I'm sure you are all invaluable to this library. I'd bet there are heaps of things I don't know that you'll have to teach me. Maybe tomorrow you can come by and show me the ropes?" Poppy was grateful her offer seemed to calm Gladys down. However, she wasn't grateful that she was now committed to spending the whole of tomorrow morning with a verifiable fruit loop.

To Poppy's surprise, the rest of the day went by uneventfully. An email from Sven let her know that he'd advertised her flat online and Carl was currently reading the applications. Sven had also added two lines of laughing face emojis to his email, which Poppy assumed were his laughing at her cockup of a morning. It was unexpectedly busy come the afternoon and Poppy had assisted most of the customers without a hitch. Gladys, who'd stuck around long after the shelving had been done, ensured Poppy was introduced to everyone as 'the new lass'.

Poppy got the impression that many of them were just there to check her out, having heard that the new librarian was in town. Mr. Jenkins had promptly–as promptly as you can when you're over the age of eighty and on a scooter–made his way to community hall to get his free tea and scone and seen it his personal business, and civic duty, to tell everyone about his shemozzle of a visit.

Poppy was grateful that the people who had borrowed books and DVDs that afternoon seemed like rational, polite humans. Even if Gladys had a story about nearly everyone of them, which she finished with 'bless them'. As if the words absolved her from gossiping.

By the time Poppy had locked the library door she felt like she'd known the regulars her whole life. She knew that Mr. Jenkins was a pain in the arse; that Arthur came in to use the computers every day to check Facebook; that Jeff had a sweet spot for Mills and Boon; Delia borrowed books for her grandson; Sandy couldn't get enough of drag queen opera; and David just came to sit. Then there were the children that came in after school to take turns at gaming on the two public computers. She also knew that Aiden Baxter didn't have a library card, which Poppy was more disappointed about than she cared to admit.

Thankfully, amongst the day's mayhem, she'd changed her phone service provider and had emergency electricity connected to the cottage. As the truck pulled into the driveway of her new home, all she could think about was washing away the day's embarrassments with a hot shower. But as she walked from the garage to the cottage backdoor a brilliant idea entered Poppy's head. Excitement of a plan unfolding grew as she skipped across to her neighbour's. *Whoever lives next door is obviously a horticultural guru. Maybe they'd like to tame my garden.* Poppy banged on the door.

A few seconds passed before she heard footsteps.

"Hullo," someone called out.

"Hi there. My name is Poppy. I live next door."

The door handle creaked open. A young man, short and round in stature appeared hesitantly. "Can I help you?" he asked slowly, diverting his eyes away from Poppy's.

"Hi," Poppy repeated with a smile. "I'm from next door. My name's Poppy."

"Hi Poppy, I'm Thomas." Thomas put his arm out straight and took Poppy's hand. He'd obviously been taught how to introduce himself.

"Nice to meet you Thomas. I've been admiring your backyard. Who does your gardening?"

"My brother isn't home until late. He's at work," Thomas interjected.

"Oh. And you're here by yourself?"

"Yes. I'm not allowed go past the gate until he gets home. But I saw you coming and knew you were the pretty lady from next door."

Poppy's cheeks warmed to a shade of beetroot. "Thanks Thomas. So your brother does he do the gardening?"

"No. I, I do the gardening. I may have Down Syndrome but I'm very independent. I'm just not allowed to use the oven."

"Oh right. Wow! You are very good at gardening Thomas. Would you be interested in helping me out in my garden? I'd pay you. It's a bit overgrown."

"Your garden is bad. Yes. I'll help you. You have to pay me twenty dollars an hour though."

"Done. When can you come over?"

"I can come over tomorrow. I'll start tomorrow. After breakfast."

"Okay Thomas, that'd be great. Have a good night and if you need anything just knock on my door."

"I'm not allowed to go past the front gate, remember?"

"Of course, sorry. I forgot. Well, I'll see you tomorrow."

"See you tomorrow." And with that Thomas closed the door.

Poppy was so excited to be getting the yard in order. She'd only been at the cottage one night but looking at the garden was already becoming unbearable. Plus, she thought, if Thomas could handle her garden, maybe he'd be interested in getting some paid work at the community hub? *Two birds, one very talented stone,* enthused Poppy.

The library didn't really have a budget. Which was odd, considering it was the start of the financial year. But, if Poppy could somehow find a way to pay Thomas to tame the gardens, she could then organise a fundraiser for any repairs, new books and replacement fire safety equipment. If she could do this, they might bring the hub up to scratch in time and save it from its grim future. Poppy made a mental note to ask Gladys about the budget tomorrow. If she had been running the library since Carmel had been on sick leave, maybe she knew where all the money had gone and why funding had been cut so extremely. Poppy knew saving the community hub in three months wasn't going to be easy. But she came to Derrin to make a difference and a difference she was going to make.

CHAPTER 10

The next morning, Poppy awoke to a hacking noise outside her bedroom window. The sound of blades sliding together momentarily merged into the dream she was having about the horrid hissing that had woken her the night before, creating a fleeting moment of panic. That was until she realised it was Thomas who had started work incredibly early. Poppy yawned. It was six o'clock in the morning and the sun was only just getting up. *How long has Thomas been out there?* The curtains framing the window that looked outside were open and Thomas' head bobbed up and down in clear sight. Clad in only her long johns and a thin thermal sweater, Poppy slid out from under the doona commando roll style. Picking up her glasses from the bedside table, she quickly pulled on her tartan dressing gown and a pair of thick socks, before creeping out of the bedroom and making her way outside.

"Good morning Thomas, you're up early," Poppy yawned, her breath frosty in the icy morning air. "Wow! You've done heaps already." Poppy couldn't believe how much Thomas had achieved. He'd hacked his way through nearly a quarter of the overgrowth, revealing paths that Poppy didn't know existed and the stumps to the cottage.

"Yep. I said I'd be over in the morning. My brother's home. He's asleep."

Poppy looked over to see a fairly new four-wheel drive dual cab ute, complete with a bull bar and spotlights, parked in the driveway next door. It was a pretty sexy car and Poppy wondered who this mysterious brother was and if he was single.

"I started at five. I will work until ten o'clock. That's five hours. You can pay me one hundred dollars in money this afternoon," confirmed Thomas, who was already turning out to be quite the businessman.

"Sure thing. I'll pop over and give it to you once I'm home from work. Will that be okay?"

"That will be okay," nodded Thomas, turning his attention back to a pile of cuttings.

"Right, well, I'll leave you to it. I've got to get ready for work." *Plus, I'm freezing to death out here.* Poppy wondered how Thomas seemed so relaxed in single digit temperatures.

"Okay. Have a good day." Thomas waved as he shoved his garden fork into the aged chicken manure he'd moved into a mound from the old disused coop.

"Thanks Thomas, you too," replied Poppy. She couldn't wait to see what the garden would look like later on this afternoon.

Gladys was waiting on the front steps of the library porch as Poppy pulled into the staff car park. She looked ready and eager with a clipboard and neatly pressed blazer. Poppy wondered if there would be time for a cup of tea before Gladys put her through her paces. There was not. For Gladys, cups of tea were strictly forbidden outside of break periods, arguing that if a hot beverage were to find itself on a book it would be sacrilege. Considering her luck with tea lately, Poppy wondered if maybe she shouldn't adopt Gladys's strict rule herself.

At 9:00 am, the library entrance was unlocked and Gladys stood there greeting every customer by name and ensuring they knew that her morning's business was to 'show Poppy the ropes'. Poppy humoured her until 11:00 am. By which time she'd learned a little less than everyone's bowel movements, including everyone's relationship status, borrowing preference, whether they had fines on their card, and who Poppy could expect to visit the library in the afternoon, but exactly nothing about the budget. In fact, every time it was mentioned Gladys waved her hand and said something about Carmel always being so generous and putting on morning teas. Poppy had also found out that Gladys's husband was the local member of parliament, Derek Batsy, who didn't have a library card. It was a brief and welcome silence when Gladys finally left the building, clipboard underarm and full of promises to bring cut flowers from her garden the next time she visited.

Not soon after Gladys had gone, a man who, judging by Gladys's description Poppy assumed was Arthur, came limping into the library with his zimmer frame. "Mornin' dear," he sang. "Beautiful day to be alive, ain't it?"

"Sure is. You must be Arthur. I'm Poppy, the new librarian. Gladys told me all about you."

Arthur snorted. "She did, did she? Batty old snoop."

Poppy could have burst out laughing at Arthur's obvious disdain for Gladys, but kept things professional. "She was very helpful. Showed me all about the workings of the library and filled me in on our customer's needs."

"I bet she did," Arthur grunted under his breath. "I'm just here to use the computer. Check my bookface or whatever it's called."

"Facebook," Poppy corrected lightly.

"What?"

"Face. Book," she repeated with a smile.

"That's it, dear," said Arthur as he trotted off to the computer.

Poppy wasn't sure he'd heard a word she'd said and was on her way over to see if he needed help when Nica bounded into the library.

"So, how's day two going?"

"Good! Great even! Gladys has given me a second and full briefing, more detailed than yesterday's, although apparently she knows nothing about the budget. It's been a busy morning. I've met heaps of locals and some travellers wanting to use the Wi-Fi too —a couple here for the rodeo, like you said. Not sure if they were looking to hook up, though. They mentioned getting into town early to set up camp and get the 'fillies' ready," Poppy laughed. "I didn't even know we had any Wi-Fi until Gladys presented a dusty old router from the cupboard out the back. She also mentioned something about a self-checkout machine that had been delivered but never installed. Turns out, Carmel thought it took away from a personalised service. Well, that's what Gladys said. I guess I'll have to put that on the to-do list as well–especially if we are to prove that this library and community hub are the cornerstone of the community. Speaking of which, the most exciting thing of all is I think I've found someone who might be interested in a bit of gardening work. I'm not sure of the logistics yet, but if he enjoys taming the yard at Page Cottage, he might just be up for doing some work here.

Help us get things into shape. What do you think?" animated Poppy, her hands out wide in a gesture of brilliance.

"Sounds great! But what about the budget? I thought there wasn't any money?"

"Well," started Poppy. "I've had another look at the figures. There may just be enough left to pay this person I have in mind. If not, I'll pay him out of my wage. It's really important that we bring the garden up to scratch. We'll need some volunteer help, though." Poppy stopped as Nica shook her head. She knew exactly what her friend was thinking. "I know, I know, Harold in the Big Toms. But just think. If I can convince a few of the vollies to help, it won't cost so much. And then when the garden is looking tiptop again, we can organise a fundraiser to fund the rest of the works. Plus, we'll do a membership drive and boost memberships. What do you say?" Poppy buzzed. She waited for Nica, who stood in silence, to confirm her genius plan.

Slowly, Nica nodded. "You know, Poppy, I think it might work! I'll help, of course, and we'll get the fellas over at the Men's Shed to pitch in repairing things. It'll be great."

"That's the spirit!" cheered Poppy, relieved that she would have Nica's creative brain to help plan the strategy.

"Hey what are you doing later?" Nica asked, changing the subject. "I'm working at the pub and there's this great band on. Why don't you come by after work?"

"I'd love to!" Poppy's eyes lit up, she couldn't remember the last time she'd gone to a gig. "I'll just have to duck home first. I have no food in the fridge and I'm sick of eating Vegemite sandwiches."

"Awesome. Look forward to seeing you there." Nica turned to leave before adding with a grin, "wear something sexy. You never know, you could meet your soul mate tonight. Remember what the tarot cards said?" she winked.

Poppy laughed. "I do. My love is someone I've already met and close by. I'm not sure I believe it but one can only hope."

"That a girl! I'll see you later."

When she got home, Poppy knocked on her neighbours' front door. The hot ute was there. Thomas should be home. He was expecting her. She knocked again. No one answered. Conscious of promising Nica she'd be at the pub before the band started, Poppy went around the back of the house to check for signs of life. She was relieved to see Thomas in the backyard with his secateurs pruning his topiary in the fading light.

"Hello Thomas. I have the money for you." She made her way past the roses trying not to snag her tight black vinyl pants and sheer lace blouse. "My backyard looks great! I can't thank you enough."

"You're welcome," Thomas said continuing to snip tiny leaves from the perfect sphere.

"Also, I don't think I properly thanked you for mowing the lawn at the cottage while no-one was living here," Poppy said teetering on the tips of her suede stilettos trying to prevent the thin heals from sinking into the ground.

"That wasn't me. That was Aiden. AIIDDDENNN." Thomas shouted over his shoulder.

Poppy's body stiffened. How many Aidens could there possibly be in Derrin?

"Yeah!" a low, gruff voice answered from somewhere in the shed.

"The lady wants to say thanks for mowing the lawn," Thomas called back.

Poppy thought she might faint. She thought about running. "Look Thomas, don't worry about it, Aiden's probably very busy." Poppy started to back away. She cursed herself for wearing heals. With every footstep she took they sucked further into the ground causing her to waddle like a duck.

"Here he comes." Thomas turned back to his pruning.

Poppy was not the only one surprised when Aiden finally emerged. He too had a look of *'oh my God'* on his face. Poppy swallowed hard. She did not expect her hot neighbour to be the man who she'd accidentally flashed her nipples to. This is why Nica had been so smug when they'd first met. She had known all along whom her neighbour was. How could she not? She knew just about every local here. Poppy made a mental note to throttle her as soon as she got to the pub.

"Um. Hi." Her heart thumped. "Thanks for, um, mowing my lawn." Poppy blushed. Her legs shook. "I mean thanks for mowing my front and back yards." *Oh shut up Poppy, you goose!*

Aiden smirked with amusement. Dressed in grease stained denim jeans and a tight white shirt, that had no chance of keeping anything about his body from the waist up a secret, he looked the type of man that belonged in a work wear calendar. He was cool, calm and collected—all the things Poppy was not. "No worries," he grinned in a way that threatened her knees. "How's it going fixing up that library? No more tea spills I hope?"

Poppy was mortified. Why did he have to go and bring up the most humiliating moment of her life? She wanted to disappear. An invisibility cloak would have been a godsend in that moment. "Ok, well, Thomas you've got the money. Thank you very much. Um will you be over tomorrow? I'm thinking maybe you'd like to help me plan some vegetable gardens. I'll pay you of course."

"Thomas is hanging out with his friends tomorrow

down at the respite centre, aren't you Thomas?" Aiden answered abruptly, his tone changing to obvious annoyance.

Thomas nodded. "I can come on the weekend."

"Mate you don't need to work. We've had this conversation."

Poppy stood awkwardly not knowing if she should say anything. Aiden's difficulty caught her off guard.

"I like working. It makes me happy. I like money." Thomas began shifting his weight on his legs. "I want to work," He repeated.

"Mate." Aiden's voice was level and direct.

"I want to work," Thomas repeated, hitting a rigid arm against the side of his body.

Aiden fanned his hands out in resignation and slapped them on his hips. A glance in her direction told Poppy her starting the conversation irritated him.

"I'll come on the weekend," Thomas smiled.

"Okay, that sounds great. I'll see you then." Poppy watched as Aiden ran his hands through his dark hair and leant against a fence post with arms crossed in front of him. His pecs flexing under his shirt as he steadied himself. His face was stern. He seemed agitated. "Enjoy your evening," she added breathlessly, peeling her eyes away and chiding herself for her inability to be sane under pressure.

"You too." Aiden replied coolly. "Watch out later.

It's supposed to rain," he winked, looking down at her blouse.

"Biceps aside, Nica, the guy is a jerk!" Poppy fumed. "I mean all I was doing was helping his brother out. He didn't have to go out of his way to make me feel uncomfortable. 'Watch out it's supposed to rain.' That was deliberate. There can't be too many employment opportunities for people with disabilities in this town and Thomas is a really talented gardener. Seriously, his topiary is amazing!"

"Hang on. Are you annoyed because he seems resistant to Thomas helping you out or because he made an obvious joke about your shirt getting wet?" Poppy could only just hear Nica over the band.

"Um, both!" It was true. Poppy still couldn't believe that Aiden had tried to convince Thomas not to do any work for her, even though he clearly wanted to. And then to back it up with an obvious jibe about her wet shirt incident riled Poppy.

Nica laughed. "Listen mate, you can't be annoyed at Aiden for making a joke—you did snout his balls. And Aiden might have his reasons for protecting his brother. Who knows? Sounds like you like the guy." Nica was being infuriatingly sensible.

"Whaaat? NO WAY. How can I like him? I've

known him for like thirty seconds. I mean, yeah, he's hot but that doesn't count for much." Poppy couldn't believe what she was hearing. The idea that she would find Aiden Baxter likeable was ridiculous. "And you don't think you could have mentioned I lived next door to the hot and grumpy fireman?"

"Okay. Yeah, sorry but I really think you two would be great together and I make it a point not to meddle. And really, if you don't like him, how come you've been talking about him non-stop for the last two hours?" Nica pointed out rather annoyingly.

"I have not!" exclaimed Poppy as she perched herself on a barstool.

"Ah, yes you have," Nica added. "I'd like to say it was the drink but you've barely touched your wine."

"Sorry, I don't really drink. Okay. You're right. Enough of the Mr. Grumpy talk. I'll shut up. The band is great. Who are they again? Their banjo set was epic."

"Death by Country. They've come to play at the rodeo." Nica's eyes sparkled. "And that guy there, I've been chatting to online." Nica waved at the drummer who winked in return.

"I thought you'd given up on men for a while?" recapped Poppy.

"I had. But I'm feeling much more myself now," Nica grinned. "Plus, I'm going to have more time on my hands come this weekend. Bob is back and itching to get behind the bar, so my stint is done."

"Hey, that's great. So glad Bob is feeling better," said Poppy, slightly distracted by the entrance of a group of lads. She looked at Nica mischievously. "Who are they?" she asked huddling into her friend.

"I know that one is Gladys's son, Charles Batsy. He's like you—from the city. Gladys said he arrived the other day and is staying for a while. Has some business in town or something." Nica pointed at a tall, well-dressed, athletic man with blonde hair. "The red headed one chatting to him is, Mattie Boyle, a fireman who works with Aiden," she continued, "and the other two, I'm not sure. Probably cowboys or stockmen here for the rodeo." Nica explained, peeling her lustful gaze from the Death by Country drummer, just long enough to fill Poppy in.

The boys swaggered across to the dance floor, drinks in hand like they owned the joint. There was an air of importance about them, especially Charles Batsy. There was something about him that intrigued Poppy. Maybe it was the fact that he was from the city, she didn't know. But she was surprised when they started walking her way. Quickly she turned toward the bar and elbowed Nica.

"What?" she said, finally breaking from her trance.

"The boys. They are coming this way." Poppy glanced briefly over her shoulder. She watched the way they joked amongst themselves and made their way to the bar.

Charles was so close Poppy could smell his aftershave. It was a spicy scent of sandalwood and patchouli that sent her hormones racing. She could practically feel the electricity pulsing from his body and wondered if he was having the same effect on Nica. Poppy didn't think so, considering her friend was still staring lustfully at her new beau. Charles was different to Aiden, thought Poppy. More refined with charisma that even the other men were drawn to. Aiden was quiet and blended in. Poppy listened to Charles' voice as he held his mates captive in conversation.

"Bugger the price of cattle mate. Did you read about the crash on the US stock exchange? Almost had a fit thinking about my investments. Do you boys have any shares in gold? I was listening to this podcast the other day that was speaking to the rate of growth in emerging industries and the power of entrepreneurship..." he continued.

Poppy didn't understand much of what Charles said but there was something about the way he said it that enthralled her. His voice was smooth and better suited to a company boardroom. It didn't have the same rough 'ocker' twang that Poppy noticed the other men out this way had. His tight moleskin trousers and perfectly pressed white collared shirt looked as though they'd never worked a day on the land in their fashionable lives.

"Hi there." Grinning, Charles leant against the bar

with his head cocked to the side and took a long casual sip of whisky.

Poppy was taken aback. She glanced at Nica who was still lost in her drummer boy. "Hi," she replied, confused as to whether or not the words were directed toward her.

Charles' blue eyes sparkled. "You don't look like you're from around here."

"Neither do you." Poppy smiled, still surprised that Charles was talking to her.

"Fair play. I'm not. I'm from Sydney. I'm just out here on business. Catching up with some old school mates who have come in for the rodeo. Not really my thing. I'm still buzzing from a week in London, just returned, but when in Rome and all that."

Poppy's head spun. The guy could talk fast. "So," he continued. "Tell me about yourself. Where have you travelled? Are you married? Children?"

"Oh gosh. My life's not that interesting," answered Poppy loudly, trying to be heard over the drum solo that was driving Nica wild next to her. "I definitely haven't just come back from London. I certainly haven't been overseas recently but in my early twenties I travelled around the world—South America, Europe, Britain that sort of thing."

"I make it a point to travel to a different country each year. I love skiing in Montana. The powder there is epic. Well tell me, what do you do for a living?"

"I'm a Librarian."

Charles perked up. "Here?" He flashed a smile. His perfect white teeth glowed in the bar lights.

"Yes. I'm here on a three-month contract. I was working in Sydney before that, in the library near to the galleries and museums down in Circular Quay." Poppy started to rub the lotus tattoo on her wrist. Why did she have to feel nervous every time an attractive man spoke to her?

"Oh yeah, I know the one. It's becoming this flashy tech hub, isn't it? Brilliant idea. So, what about the other questions? Are you married? Do you have children?"

Poppy felt like she was being interviewed. "No, I'm not married, I don't have children and I don't really think the tech hub is such a great idea. Not when it takes over the entire library, anyway."

"Do you want them? Children and a husband, I mean? An attractive woman like yourself, petite, well groomed, beautiful long dark hair, I'm surprised you're single."

"Um yeah, maybe, if it's the right person at the right time. My focus would be on a great relationship first. And who's saying I'm not single by choice?"

"I like the way you think." Charles sucked in his bottom lip. He stared at her intensely and Poppy felt herself move into some sort of trance. "Can I buy you a drink?" he asked smoothly. "I'm Charles Batsy. Forgive me for not introducing myself already but I like to sum a girl up before giving her my name."

Poppy wasn't sure whether she should be flattered or not. Charles was obviously a man who knew what he wanted, and she wondered what he wanted with Derrin? It surely wasn't to chat to her, but she was flattered anyway. There was something about Charles that captivated her. Something about his confidence, the way he grinned when he recalled a memory or told her something about himself. He was charming and smelt so good it made Poppy tingle in places that hadn't tingled for a very long time.

By the time last drinks were being called, Nica had long disappeared with the drummer and Poppy had spent a whole three hours drinking soda water and listening to Charles chat about his international travels and life in Sydney.

"So, tell me what you do exactly. Professionally, I mean?" Poppy asked Charles as they walked through the darkened car park.

"Let's just say I work in developing vibrant community living spaces," dismissed Charles.

"That's so interesting. I'm totally into that. I love the idea of green urban spa..." Charles' body was in front of her. Warmth radiated from it. She noticed the way his breath steamed. Poppy, who was genuinely interested in the topic, paused.

"Shhh. Stop talking." He whispered. Poppy

stumbled as Charles pulled her waist into his hips and pressed his lips against hers. She felt her knees buckle as his tongue glided momentarily into her mouth—the sensation over in a split second. "I have to go back to the hotel and check my email. I will pick you up after work tomorrow. Say five o'clock." Charles didn't wait for an answer. Instead, he gave Poppy a wink and jumped into the shiny Land Rover that Poppy hadn't even realised they were standing next to. Speechless, she watched as he drove off into the night.

By the time Poppy jumped in the shower the next morning, she had long forgotten about the attractive bicep laden Aiden. She didn't care if he was next door. She was still revealing in last night's steamy, albeit unexpected, kiss with Charles and was feeling good about the day ahead. That was until a God almighty screech caused her to jump and knock her head on the tiny shower shelf. "What the actual F!"

Pulling back the shower curtain revealed nothing, yet Poppy could have sworn the screeching was coming from within the steamy room. This was the third time now she'd heard coarse shrieking. Carmel had mentioned nothing about the cottage being inhabited. *Maybe it's a possum?* Poppy prayed not. She'd read stories about the seemingly cute creatures keeping

households up all night by making a ruckus on roofs and
scrapping in the backyard.

With a towel around her, Poppy ventured into the
hall to investigate. She felt unusually brave and
wondered if, after two short days, the country was
starting to permeate her blood. What she wasn't
expecting to see was a large, mangy black creature
making its way into the kitchen. Poppy froze. She had a
cat. Or rather, the cottage did. Either way, it acted like it
owned the joint.

The cat was just about as impressed as Poppy was to
see it. "Here kitty, kitty," Poppy coaxed, wondering how
it had gotten in. "Here kitty kitty." The cat cowered
under the kitchen bench, hissing with bare teeth and
heckles up. Poppy wasn't entirely sure what to do. In an
amateur manoeuvre, she reached out her hand as a
gesture of friendship. The next three seconds were a
blur that ended with more hissing, clambering,
screaming and Poppy landing on her back in the kitchen
with an undignified thud.

She would have been happy to board up the house
and move into town but as luck would have it, it was
then that Aiden, banged on the kitchen window.

"Woah! I'll give you a minute," Aiden laughed as he
ducked out of view.

Wide-eyed, he looked just as shocked as she did.
Except he wasn't stark naked and splayed on the floor,
having just lost a battle with a comparatively small

creature. Poppy grappled for the towel. She hadn't shaved 'down-there' in nearly two years—and her pubes were so long they'd given themselves their own trendy balayage. "It was a cat!" she squealed.

Covering herself she hid from view of the kitchen window. Why did Aiden's presence always result in her wanting a huge sinkhole to gobble her up?

"Oh Yeah. That's Mr. Meow. He was a feral kitten Carmel rescued from the shelter. He's pretty wild. Been around here a bit lately looking for food. He and Thomas are great mates. You have been feeding him, haven't you?" Aiden asked from the side of the house.

"*No,*" exasperated Poppy. "How did he even get in?"

"There's a cat flap in the back door." Aiden replied as if it was common knowledge.

"Of course," Poppy grunted.

"Okay... well I just thought I'd make sure you hadn't injured yourself—that was one hell of a racket before. I heard it over the fence."

Poppy heard Aiden's footsteps disappear down her drive and back over to next door. She slumped against the wall, her body covered in the type of red blotchy rash one gets when they are about to die from embarrassment. Poppy couldn't help but feel she'd treated Aiden badly. He had only been checking to see if she was okay. And although, Poppy had been embarrassed she knew she could have been politer to him.

Poppy knocked hesitantly on Aiden's front door. She knew he was inside. Indie folk music could be heard playing softly in the background. She was just about to give up when the doorknob turned. Aiden stood shirtless in front of her in football shorts with sweat beading down his chest and a towel over his shoulder.

Poppy waited as he wiped the cloth over his face and took a swig from his drink bottle. She watched the way his Adam's apple moved up and down with every gulp. Sweat glistened under his eyes and clung to his five o'clock shadow.

"What's up?" he asked abruptly. Poppy wondered if he'd already blocked the image of her overgrown vagina out of his mind. "I was just in the middle of a workout."

"Look, Aiden. I'm so sorry about the way things have started off between us. I feel like such a goose. You must think me mad. I pretty much assaulted you on Tuesday and now you've had the unpleasant luck of seeing me spread eagled on the kitchen floor. I am so sorry."

Aiden stared at her, his expression deadpan. "You know what. Don't worry about it." Poppy turned to leave thinking that Aiden probably had seen enough of her to last his lifetime. "Wait!"

Charges of electricity surged up her spine as Aiden's fingers brushed against her skin. "Look. It's okay. I've been a jerk," he said letting her hand fall to her waist. "I'm sorry. I wasn't that polite to you when you asked me about phone reception on Monday. I'd just come off a shift, and we had a pretty nasty car accident to deal with, some out of towners driving too fast in a BMW, I was fatigued and not really up for polite chit chat. When I realised you were from the city, it kinda got my back up. I'm sorry if I came across as rude," Aiden offered earnestly.

"It can't be easy," Poppy offered empathetically. "If anyone's to apologise, it really should be me. I mean I made such a balls up of the maintenance inspection." Poppy wondered why Aiden was smirking and then realised what she'd said. "I didn't mean it like that!" she blushed.

"I know," Aiden laughed, his dimples showing in his cheeks. "A guy like me should be lucky having a fine lady such as yourself so close to his fishing tackle. It's been a while since a woman was that close to the region," he chuckled.

Poppy felt her cheeks burn. She wasn't sure if Aiden was flirting or not. Surely, someone as hot as Aiden Baxter, had women falling all over him.

"We got to get ready Aiden. Hello, Poppy," said Thomas, walking out of the house.

"Oh right," Poppy remembered that today was the day Thomas went to his respite group.

"No worries, buddy," replied Aiden, before turning

back to her. "I've got to go. But I'm sure we'll be seeing each other soon."

Poppy wasn't sure why she felt disappointed as she walked back to her cottage. She hadn't expected any grand gestures of friendship or promises of catch-ups but there was something in Poppy that had wanted to find out more about her new neighbour. There was something about him that intrigued Poppy and although she felt nervous as hell and classically unstable around him, Poppy wanted to spend more time with him. Somehow, he felt homely.

CHAPTER 11

Poppy felt the truck vibrate underneath her as she chugged into town. Even with two coats, a scarf and woollen tights, she still felt cold. And every few seconds she had to wipe the fog from her glasses. She couldn't wait to get to the library and thaw out. She wondered how Thomas was able to garden in such early morning temperatures. The ground must feel like ice. As she pulled into the car park her phone lit up beside her. It was Rachel. She was surprised that this was the first time Rachel had messaged Poppy since she'd gained phone reception the day before.

After ensuring the park brake was securely on, Poppy tapped on the message.

OMG!!! Sis. Pops

Are you there?

I think Chris is cheating on me!!!

Poppy couldn't believe what she was reading. Chris and Rachel were solid. Poppy knew Chris had been working long hours but she would never in a million years have believed he was having an affair. No sooner had she unlocked the backdoor to the library and put her bag down, Poppy picked up her phone and called her sister.

It went straight to message bank.

This wasn't like Rachel. Poppy tried once more. No answer. This time she left a message. "Hi Rach. What's going on? Tried to call you a couple of times. I'm sure Chris isn't seeing anyone. I just don't believe it." Poppy hung up. She was really worried about Rachel. She hadn't been herself lately. Could this be the reason she was so emotional about Poppy leaving for a few months to work in the country? Had she suspected her husband of ten years was cheating on her this whole time? Poppy picked up her phone to try calling Rachel again but was interrupted by a knocking on the workroom window. It was Nica.

Pushing a trolley load of books to be deleted out of the way, Poppy heaved the bottom of the double hung window up and poked her head out. "Morning lover girl," Poppy winked. "How did you go last night and why are you knocking on my window?"

Nica went all dreamy. "Last night was *fabulous*. Oh

my gosh, talk about a man who knows his rhythm," she giggled. "And I'm knocking on the window because I'm not coming in, I've got to go and get ready for this morning's printing with clay tiles workshop."

"Well, well. Did he hit you with his 'rhythm stick'?" Poppy couldn't help herself. She knew it was funny and thankfully Nica cracked up laughing but not for the same reason.

"That song is about a disability, you numpty, not a penis!" she said, rolling her eyes.

"Wait. What? Really?" Poppy could have sworn the lyrics screamed 'sex'.

"Speaking of—just quickly—I noticed you were talking to a certain suave someone last night?" Nica raised her eyebrows inviting Poppy to dish the goss.

"Nothing happened. Charles basically chewed my ear off and talked about how great his life in the city and the snow in Montana is. And then he told me that he'd pick me up this afternoon after work for a drink." Poppy felt like last night had been a bit of a whirlwind. Chatting to Charles Batsy was a bit like hearing a resume. He seemed a nice enough, but Poppy wondered if she really wanted to go for another drink. He hadn't so much as asked her but just assumed she had wanted to. Was the guy really that used to getting any girl he wanted, thought Poppy? "To be honest, Nica, Charles seems an alright guy, but I've got other things on my mind. I need to get out and meet the rest of the volunteers and figure out what sort of fund raiser will bring in enough money to get this joint up the scratch."

"Well, today's Thursday, why don't you come over to the art studio on your lunch break and I'll take you over to the Men's Shed, introduce you to the lads there?"

"That'd be great!" Poppy couldn't wait to meet the other members of the community hub. "I want to organise a meeting with everyone next week sometime to discuss how we are going to go about fixing this place up. We don't have much time and the more I think about it, the more there is to do."

"Sounds awesome. Okay, I'll see you at lunchtime," Nica confirmed.

"Sure thing." Just then Rachel's name flashed up on Poppy's phone. "I've got to go but I'll defs see you later." Poppy picked up the call as she waved Nica goodbye.

"Rach! What the heck is going on?"

Poppy could hear Rachael sobbing down the other end of the phone. "I found a mobile number in his pants pocket."

"That could mean anything," Poppy said as she moved through the library space turning on lights and flicking on the public computers.

"It had lipstick on it," cried Rachel. "And he's been acting really funny lately. Working long hours. And apparently, he has to work all this weekend. He's barely even seen Ben!"

"Well maybe he just has a lot on. Have you asked him directly?"

"Yes. And he tells me not to be so stupid," wept Rachel.

Poppy wasn't sure of what to say. If Rachel wasn't exaggerating, it sounded odd. "Why don't you and Ben come here for a few nights? The change of scenery might do you both the world of good. Plus, the rodeo is on this Friday. Ben would love that."

"Maybe."

"Oh come on. What else are you going to do? At least you'll feel good about being out of the house. You can meet my friend Nica and help me come up with some ideas to raise money to fix the library."

"What's wrong with the library?" Rachel sniffled, finally calming down.

"A lot. Look, I'll explain it to you when you get here." Poppy said goodbye to her sister and put down the phone. She wasn't sure she could take any more dramas. With the pressure of saving the community hub and now her sister's marriage, Poppy wasn't sure that moving to the country was going to end up being the picture-perfect idyllic escape she'd hoped for.

Luckily, the rest of the morning went by without a hitch or emergency phone call. Poppy was still worried, though. She hadn't given Charles her number and wanted to know if he was still taking her out for drinks that night. She didn't have to wonder for long. As Poppy closed the library for her lunch break, she noticed Charles, dressed very dapper in a navy-blue suit, standing street side in front of the community hub. He had a folder tucked under his arm and was chatting to two other businessmen. Poppy was curious what it was they were shaking hands on. She waited for them to part before calling out to Charles.

"Hiya!"

"Poppy." Charles looked slightly uncomfortable and surprised to see her. "How's the day going?" he asked leaning in for a hug.

"Great," Poppy lied. Charles didn't need to know about her nudist 'trip' or sister's phone call. "Do you usually hold business meetings on the street?" she asked casually.

"Ha. No. That was just a conversation with some mates. You know how it is in the business world. Networking and all that." Charles fidgeted, before quickly changing the subject. "So. Drinks tonight? Also, you should probably give me your number."

Feeling like it would be rude to back out now, Poppy nodded. "You should know though, I don't really drink.

So maybe just a quick one would be good. It's a school night, after all."

Charles laughed. "Come on. Every night's a Friday night for a city girl."

Poppy didn't have the nerve to admit to Charles that she hadn't been out after dark on a Friday in over two years. And the last time she had, she'd been home by 10:30 pm for a hot chocolate. "Okay, well, just a couple won't hurt." Poppy forced a smile and typed her number into Charles' phone. She had barely handed it back to him before he was on it again and waving goodbye.

"See you later," she added, uselessly.

Nica's studio was amazing. Poppy couldn't help but walk around and repeat the words 'wow', 'awesome' and 'cool'. The space was walled with unstained pine shelving and benches ran lengthways in the middle of the room. Tin cans, filled with tools, sat in the middle of the tables like flower vases and students' artwork adorned the shelves. Poppy listened as Nica explained about the different phases of drying and when the works would be ready to be fired.

"That's what we call heating the clay up to a temperature that makes it hard," Nica explained. Poppy was intrigued by how glazes went in the kiln one colour and came out completely different. It was magical alchemy, as Nica had poetically put it.

What Poppy couldn't help but notice was that some of the panels of corrugated iron, that clad the studio were rusted and in dire need of repair. Poppy wondered how long the community hub had been going downhill for. "Hey Nica, when did things start getting overgrown and in such bad shape around here?"

Poppy waited as Nica stopped to think for a second. "Um, well I guess probably around the same time that Harold died."

"That explains the garden. But what about the buildings?"

"Well, I reckon things probably started going downhill when Carmel took sick leave. She left very abruptly, at which point good old Gladys stepped up. I think Gladys was just bored, actually. Her and Derek were active grey nomads, but when Derek was elected local MP. she started doing all this volunteer work, especially, around here. Not that you'd think anything got done, judging by the state of things."

"So let me get this straight. Derek Batsy gets elected MP. Around about the same time, Carmel mysteriously goes on extended sick leave. Gladys starts volunteering, neigh running, this place and now it's no longer passing fire and safety inspections because what funding there is hasn't been used on proper maintenance."

"Yes."

"Something isn't right. Nica, this is serious. We need to raise the money and bring this building up to scratch or it's at real risk of being decommissioned. I need to chat to the guys at the Men's Shed. Can we go over there now? My lunch break will be over soon and we have to organise a hub meeting about this a.s.a.p."

"Yeah no worries. Let's go now. I really hope we can do something, Poppy. This place really is needed in the community. It has so much potential."

Poppy followed Nica as she set foot through the overgrown weed patch and into the Men's Shed. A small, stout man, looked up as they walked through the open door. The lathe he was working at slowed to a halt as he removed his earmuffs. "Who have we here, Nica?" he asked, walking forward with a smile so big it reminded Poppy of the Cheshire Cat from Alice and Wonderland.

"Tony, this is Poppy, the new librarian," said Nica, turning to Poppy. "Tony manages the group," she added.

Poppy took Tony's generous handshake in her own. "It's so lovely to meet you."

"Likewise," he added warmly. "Let me introduce you to the others."

Poppy took turns in shaking the hands of Donald, who was the group's newest member and was working on a dollhouse for his granddaughter, Steve, who had been fixing tools for friends for the last three years and, Clive who enjoyed making puzzles for members of the local aged care facility and who Poppy thought looked like Santa Claus. "It's such an honour to meet you all!" Poppy spent the next few minutes listening to the men talk about their projects and what 'The Shed', as they called it, meant to them.

"Ever since my wife died, it gives me purpose. A place to come and have a chat," Clive said honestly. "My wife had dementia and died in the nursing home last year. I guess that's why I make the puzzles for the residents, to give back. It's a bit of a prison in there with nothing to do." The other men nodded.

Poppy felt now was the right time to ask them if they'd be willing to make the time to meet with her next week. "Gentlemen, I'm wondering if you might have time to meet with me next Thursday? There are some things I need to discuss with you about this place and the community hub in general. The safety standards haven't been met and Council and the local fire department have given us a deadline to get it done. I have some ideas but I'm going to need everyone's help. What do you say to next Thursday evening? We can meet at the library after it closes." Poppy sat next to Nica who had remained silent this whole time and waited for the four men, who chatted briefly amongst themselves. Poppy was glad they were considering the matter with such weight. It wasn't long before one of them spoke.

"Forgive us love," said Steve very seriously. "We

have a cards night on that Thursday and had to work out a new date before accepting." Poppy could feel Nica roll her eyes. "But we'd love to meet you. We've been saying ourselves we need to do something about this place or next thing you know it'll be bulldozed while we're still sitting at the banding saws."

Poppy laughed nervously. "I'll see you all next Thursday then."

"Are you going to invite the library volunteers?" Asked Nica as they walked back through the garden and into the library.

"I probably should. I'm sure they'd love to help get this place back in shape. They might be useful for the membership drive I plan on doing." Poppy sounded willing but for some reason she had doubt that including the other volunteers would be a good thing. She hadn't met Jenny or Claris, so it wasn't about them, but there was something about Gladys that didn't sit right with Poppy and she couldn't put her finger on what it was. As head librarian, Poppy had to find a way to include the volunteers, especially when she would be consulting the other members of the community hub. She resolved to continue to try to find out why the library and community hub were in the state they were.

CHAPTER 12

Poppy rubbed her hands together. It was almost dark, and she was sure the temperature had to be in the single digits. She had been waiting half an hour on the front porch of the library for Charles to show up. He was late. She was just about to give up and go home when Aiden's ute pulled up in the customer car park.

"Hey!" he greeted with an open smile, as he jumped out from the driver's seat. "I was just on my way home from work. I thought you would have left by now. Everything okay?"

"Everything's okay, thanks. I was just waiting for someone." Even though Poppy wasn't really looking forward to another late night, she couldn't help but feel disappointed Charles had stood her up. "I was just about to leave."

"You look like you're dressed up to go out. You look

nice. Where are you headed?" asked Aiden as he shut the wire mesh gate to the hub behind him. He was still in his uniform and Poppy found it hard to focus on anything other than how good he looked.

"I'm supposed to be meeting a friend for a drink. But something must have happened. I'm thinking I might just go home, instead."

"Nah. Don't do that," Aiden said, unusually jovial. "I'll shout you a drink, if you're up for it? Give me a chance to apologise for acting like a general tosser and being an arse about Thomas. What do you say?" Aiden's dimpled cheeks made it hard to say no, and Poppy reckoned he knew it.

"Okay, but I don't really drink," she warned.

"Perfect, because I was honest when I told you I didn't either. How about you come around and have a very strong soda water at mine. Thomas will be there but we can sit on the porch and chat while he watches his evening shows."

"You know what? That actually sounds perfect. Let me just duck home quickly and I'll knock on your door in about fifteen minutes. How does that sound?"

"No worries at all. See you soon." Aiden smiled and turned and walked back through the gate. Poppy waved him off as he reversed out of the car park and drove down the road. She was grateful for the change of plans and the fact that, just now, was the first time she had finally felt at ease in Aiden's presence, she hadn't flashed anything, fallen over anything or stuttered over anything and Poppy was glad.

She had all but forgotten about Charles' no show when her phone beeped.

Hey sexy. Sorry about this afternoon. Got held up at a meeting. Hope you didn't wait around. I'm free later tonight. I can meet you at yours.

Poppy couldn't work out if Charles was lining up another drinks date or a booty call. She wanted neither. There was something about him that was undeniably charismatic, but Poppy couldn't help but feel that he was the sort of guy that would have girls lined up on speed dial, waiting to go.

Hi there, I waited for a bit but figured you'd been held up.

I've been invited to a friend's house so not available later. Enjoy your night.

Happy with her message, Poppy dropped her phone back in her pocket and headed to the truck. By the time she finally got in, the steering wheel and seat were frozen. She was looking forward to sharing Aiden's company for a couple of hours and was thankful that she'd stopped off at the grocers this morning on the way to work to pick up cat food and a few basic supplies. She'd do a proper shop before Rachel and Ben arrived.

Poppy still couldn't believe that Chris could be having an affair. Anyone who'd met him would have sworn his fidelity and Rachel was awesome, even if a little high maintenance.

The drive back to the cottage was a quick one. Poppy parked in the shed and eagerly bounded up the back steps. Carefully, she looked around. *No exploding kitties, awesome.* She walked into the kitchen and put the shopping bags on the bench. She'd unpack them later. Taking her phone out of her pocket, she made her way into the lounge and quickly built the fire. She felt chuffed about her ability to warm herself. *At least it will be cozy when I get back.* She smiled to herself as the flames grew. With the fire started, she bounded out the front door.

It was just after six o'clock when Poppy knocked on Aiden and Thomas's front door. She could hear the television on in the lounge as she waited for it to open. Thomas must have been watching something hilarious because every few seconds she could hear him laugh so hard it made her giggle. She was in the middle of a chuckle when Aiden opened the door.

"Why good evening, fancy seeing you here. What's so funny?" he beamed.

"It's Thomas. I can't help but enjoy his laughter," grinned Poppy.

"Oh yeah. He loves that home animal video show, or whatever it's called. It's the one that used to be on the telly when we were kids. Still cracks me up, actually. I love the ones with guinea pig, I find them really funny." Poppy listened to Aiden as she followed him through the house and into the kitchen. The floor plan was almost identical to her cottage, and Aiden had decorated in a modern Scandinavian style. It was gorgeous, light greys, white trim, dark stained timber floorboards with natural fibre furniture and accessories. And whatever was cooking smelled amazing. The air wafting down the hall was so thick with the scent of herbs and spices Poppy could have eaten it.

"Can I smell coriander and kefir lime?" she salivated.

"Good pickup. I'm cooking Thai basil stir-fry. It's Thomas's favourite. You're welcome to join us."

"Hello Poppy," Thomas called down the hall.

"It must be an ad break," smiled Aiden. "He's got selective hearing when the show's playing."

"Hi Thomas!" Poppy called back. "How are you?" There was no reply. "It must be back on," she joked.

"So what would you like to drink? Soda water with lemon, soda water with lime or soda water with soda water?"

"Ooh exciting selection," teased Poppy, "I think I'll have a soda water with lemon."

"Coming right up." Aiden moved effortlessly around the kitchen. Poppy watched as he placed two glass tumblers on the bench and squeezed lemon into both before pouring over the fizzy liquid. Turning off the heat to the wok, he handed her a drink and called down the hall to Thomas. "Just sitting on the back porch, mate." Aiden nodded his head toward the back door and motioned for Poppy to go before him. "It's cold out, but I have the heaters on."

Poppy opened the door for Aiden who flicked on the light.

"Oh Aiden, this is beautiful." Poppy was taken aback by how cozy the sitting area was. The porch was decorated in sparkling fairy lights, lanterns and big comfy chevron cushions. The heaters glowed, and it was surprisingly warm.

"Take a cushion," Aiden offered. Poppy watched him sit effortlessly on the ground.

"Wow, you're pretty flexible for a muscly guy."

Aiden laughed. "Thanks. I do yoga, most days. And meditate. In my, job you kinda need to use all the tools you can."

Poppy nodded. "I'm a trained yoga and meditation teacher myself. Did it ages ago. I only taught for a year but the knowledge has never left me. It's pretty powerful stuff."

"I noticed your tattoo the other day, at the library. The lotus. I like it. It's feminine." The way Aiden's eyes traced her arm and landed on her wrist sent tingles down Poppy's spine.

"Thanks, I got it when I graduated, just before I left the training school in Bali."

"That's really cool. Maybe you can teach me a few poses?"

"I'm not sure how much more I'd know than you but, sure, if there's anything I can help with." Poppy nestled into the cushions and helped herself to a mustard yellow throw. "So, tell me about yourself. How did you come to be in Derrin?" she asked lifting the glass to her lips. The tiny bubbles popped against her nose as she took a sip.

"I grew up here," Aiden replied. "I did move away for a while after uni. I studied marine biology then got a job up in Cairns with a research project. I had a girlfriend up there, so it seemed like a good idea at the time. When that ended, I came back home to be close to Thomas. a few mates were still here, one of them is in my fire crew, Mattie Boyle. That's when I decided to change careers and try out for the Emergency Services. I didn't want to be a cop, or an ambo, so fireman was the best thing, plus Mattie had already made selection. What about you?"

"I grew up in Sydney. I haven't lived anywhere else, which is a bit embarrassing at thirty-two." Poppy thought it sweet that Aiden brushed away this fact with a wave of his hand as if to suggest it no big deal. "I loved growing up in the city, and all my family are there, but I never really felt like it was home. I've spent most of my adult life wander-lusting over books and magazines about country living, but this is the first time I've lived anywhere rural."

"What is it you love about the country?" Aiden asked earnestly as he dropped back on his elbows. The sight of his muscular body clad in jeans, woollen socks and a dark green cable knit jumper did something to Poppy's neurology that caused her to lose focus for just a second.

"Um, well it's green, the fresh air is nice, the people are friendly, there are animals, I can't really put it into words. Ever since I was a kid the idea of living somewhere surrounded by farmland and not skyscrapers has been my dream. And I know it's silly because I've only been here for three days and I'm not staying long, but there's something about Derrin, that feels like home." It was hard to describe, but ever since Poppy had stepped foot off the train, she'd felt like she belonged.

"The country is awesome," agreed Aiden. "It's hard sometimes, Cold, dry, rainy, snowy, but you're right, the people are friendly, minus this old grumpy fireman," Aiden laughed. The deep timbre tones of his chuckle had a calming effect and Poppy couldn't believe that it wasn't long ago she'd thought he didn't like her. She was grateful for how easy the conversation flowed between the two of them. She felt like she could curl up and chat to Aiden all night.

Poppy fell silent for a second. "Is your job very hard?"

Aiden stared into the night. "Sometimes," he replied sombrely, "and sometimes it's just a whole shift of paper pushing, hours of doing not much and catching up on admin. Mostly, I enjoy it. It can be hard with car accidents though. You never really get used to seeing a bad one of those." Poppy watched as Aiden drew in a deep breath. "You see, that's how my parents died, and I ended up as sole guardian of Thomas."

"Oh Aiden, I'm so sorry. I had no idea." Without thinking Poppy reached out and put her hand on Aiden's. She felt him flinch slightly. She pulled away worried she was being too informal.

"They were driving back to Derrin after visiting their friends in Sydney. It was raining really heavily and an oncoming road train blinded them. They swerved and lost control of the vehicle. Hit a tree going eighty kilometres an hour. We were called to the job. The boys at coms didn't know the victims were my parents. There are no words to describe seeing your loved ones like that." Aiden paused and stared into the night. Turning his face from Poppy's, he cleared his throat. "You never get over it," his voice shook.

Poppy was lost for words. She wanted to hold Aiden and take away his pain. She had never lost a loved one let alone holding graphic memories of their last moments. Just the thought of losing Rachel caused a lump to form in Poppy's throat. She listened as Aiden continued.

"Thomas was only ten and was staying at our grandma's place for the night. She was alive then but passed soon after Mum and Dad died. The heartbreak was too much. I've been in Derrin ever since. We love it here and it's good for Thomas to be in a town he knows. His meeting you has done him the world of good. I'm sorry I was such a pain in the arse. I just struggle to let go. I'm worried that if he goes off and does things on his own, he'll get hurt and I won't be there to look out for him."

"I'm so sorry you had to experience that, Aiden," Poppy shook her head, feeling Aiden's grief. "It's truly heartbreaking."

"It is," he repeated, "thanks for listening. I'm usually not such a morbid bugger. I just felt like I wanted you to know why I overreach on Thomas wanting to do things for himself. I didn't want you to think I was controlling, or anything like that."

"Thanks for sharing with me. It can't be an easy story to tell." Poppy could see there was still emotion in Aiden's eyes. For a moment, they both stared into the darkness, listening to a plover's distant call and frogs sing in unison. Poppy could feel the electricity pulsating from Aiden's body. She didn't dare touch him again, though every inch of her wanted to. Badly. The thought was almost too much to bare, and she wondered if he could feel the intensity too. Every-so-often she caught his eyes sparkling in her direction.

Poppy could have sat on the porch next to Aiden forever, but it was Thomas who broke the silence.

"Shows over Aiden. Can we have dinner, please?"

Aiden smiled and picked up his glass. "Duty calls," he mused. "Are you staying for dinner, we'd love to have you?"

Poppy didn't want to go home, but she was exhausted. It had been a hectic first few days in Derrin, and it was catching up with her. "I'd love to stay, really. The food smells amazing. But I'd probably fall asleep on my plate," she said yawning.

Aiden didn't press the point. Poppy knew that as a shift worker, he would understand fatigue. "Let me put together a doggy bag quickly, so at least you don't have to cook when you get home." Aiden disappeared into the kitchen before Poppy could protest. By the time she had finished saying goodbye to Thomas, he'd returned with a stainless-steel bento box of stir-fry, coconut rice, Thai salad and grapes. Poppy thought the grapes a nice touch. As she waved goodbye one last time, Poppy's heart was full. Spending time with Aiden had been like hanging out with a long and trusted friend.

Poppy ate quickly while watching the fire burn down and waiting for the elusive Mr. Meow to show up. He did not. This didn't really bother Poppy. She figured that Mr. Meow had been looking after himself for quite some time and could do so for one more night. Plus, she was too consumed by thoughts of Aiden to care much about an angry cat. Staring into the flames, Poppy fantasised about their conversation, wanting to relive every detail, until her eyelids finally got the better of her.

CHAPTER 13

Come morning, Poppy awoke to a stream of notifications on her mobile. There were a few messages from Rachel, an email from Sven and a message from Mitch. Poppy opened Mitch's first.

> Poppy, how are ya? The place has gone balls up since you've left. Didn't take long. Merle has retired, and Gabby is officially dating Daniel although I'm not sure he sees it like that. She will not shut up. I reckon you'd get your job back it you wanted it? Pleeeaaassse come back! Mitch.

Poppy wasn't surprised that the changes had caused Merle to leave but what did surprise her was acknowledging that she didn't care. She had only been out of the city a few short days but already she felt like it had been a lifetime. She already cared so much for her new friends, the community hub and the town that she couldn't see herself ever leaving. Poppy knew that time would come eventually and three months would go by quickly but she couldn't go back, not yet and not before she saved the community hub.

> Hey Mitch, Wow Gabby and Daniel, hey? That's a surprise. Sad about Merle leaving but I can see why the changes aren't for her. She'll love retirement. Derrin is really great. I love being in a smaller community. Thanks for the message and happy Friday, Poppy.

Sven had emailed to tell her he'd found someone to sublet her flat, a lovely young lady in her late twenties who made raw vegan cakes for a living. Sven and Carl, who were lovers of all sweet things, reiterated that everything was under control and Poppy needn't rush back if she loved it out there. They also wanted to know if she'd gotten over her embarrassing moment with Aiden and met any handsome eligible bachelors. She decided not to reply with any details. She couldn't afford for Sven to become too excited, he'd be planning a wedding before she'd even got to second base.

Poppy was hesitant to open Rachel's text. She braced herself for hundreds of sobbing faces emojis, but was quite taken aback as she started to read her sister's message. Rachel had had a complete turnaround and seemed quite perky.

> Hola sis, I will arrive in Derrin this afternoon around the time you finish work. Ben is staying with a friend for the weekend. I need girl time. Re: Chris I've decided I'm fabulous and if he is cheating, he's a bastard and I'll remarry someone rich. Ciao xo

Poppy felt exhausted already. She knew what her sister was like when she let her hair down and it was *not* pretty. In fact, it was rather vulgar. The last time Rachel drank, Poppy had needed to stop her from getting into a catfight with a barmaid who'd emptied her glass too early. This was before having to hold up Rachel's skirt as she peed beside the Sydney Opera House. Poppy hoped like hell that Rachel was planning on having a quiet one but considering she didn't have Ben to look after it was safe to assume she wasn't.

Grabbing her car keys, Poppy shoved her phone in her bag and began to walk out of the cottage. The rodeo was her first community shindig and the excitement of the event had given her an idea on how to raise enough money to save the library and community hub. There were still so many unanswered questions — mainly, why did it need saving in the first place, but Poppy had resigned herself to the fact that the 'why' didn't really matter. If she could raise the money to action the maintenance report, boost the membership and the amount of people using the spaces, then she would have the proof that it was viable. Council would have no reason to decommission it.

Town was busy, even at eight-thirty that morning. Four-wheel drives and horse floats lined the streets. The bakery was so busy there was a line down the pavement. Poppy yawned. She'd hoped there would be enough time to grab a cuppa before work. Driving down Cock Ball Street she noticed a coffee cart pulled up outside the train station. The cute flamingo-pink vintage caravan was a bright oasis with its blue bunting and beautifully lettered chalkboard signs. They sold everything from chai lattes to spiced coffee and old-fashioned cake doughnuts. The smell had Poppy hooked as soon as she'd jumped out of the truck. Walking back up the street from the library to the coffee cart, Poppy felt like she was noticing the town for the first time, all over again. She realised she'd been so busy since arriving she hadn't even had time to take a look around. Having Rachel stay would be the perfect excuse to get out and about this weekend and explore the wintery landscape. Nica had mentioned that there were wineries and boutique breweries close by and Poppy was looking forward to sampling some local drops.

Standing in line with a pottery keep-cup she'd

bought yesterday from the supermarket, Poppy felt excited about the months ahead. She wondered if the people standing in front of her were locals or visitors in town for the rodeo. Poppy was lost in her thoughts, until a loud and deliberate cough hit her from behind.

"Charles! Fancy seeing you here. How was your night last night?" Poppy was still a bit miffed about being stood up but didn't want Charles to know it. He was dressed in another perfectly tailored suit; different to the one he wore yesterday. His face was smooth, and his eyebrows were clipped to perfection. Poppy thought for sure he'd buffed his nails.

"Yeah, sorry about that," he replied just loud enough that everyone around them could hear. "It's business you know. I figured it wouldn't be such a big deal and you'd have other plans. I'll expect to be able to buy you a drink at the rodeo tonight. I don't usually go to these sorts of things, but my mates have twisted my arm. Ah almond latte for me thank you and a—what are you having Poppy?" he asked smoothly.

"A chai latte please but I can get my own."

Not listening to a word Poppy said, Charles whipped out his phone and paid with a tap of his mobile. "Thanks beautiful," he said to the young lady who was taking the orders, before whispering into Poppy's ear "let's see if the coffee's as good as in the city."

"I'm sure it'll be fine," Poppy said as she handed over her keep cup.

"So, are you going to the rodeo with anyone?" asked Charles.

"Just my sister. And I have a friend going."

"Perfect. Then you're coming with me."

Before Poppy could protest, Charles had organised to pick her and Rachel up from Page Cottage at six o'clock. By the time their drinks were ready Poppy was feeling like five minutes of silence would be a wonderful thing. Charles loved to talk and primarily about himself. He was adamant about escorting her back to the library and Poppy felt he would never leave her alone. Luckily his phone rang just as they were walking away from the coffee van. Charles, who apologised casually, dashed off on account of some business emergency, mentioning something about dropping over later to check the place out. Poppy had no idea what he meant.

It was just before 9:00 am when Poppy had finished turning on the computers and straightening the shelves. A knock on the door alerted her to it being opening time and Poppy hoped that her day would be a cruisy one. She was delighted when she opened the entrance door to find Aiden and Thomas smiling on the front steps waiting eagerly.

"Good morning," they both chimed, in a way that

brought an instant smile to her face. "We've come to get library cards," Aiden beamed. "I haven't had one since I was a kid. I'm pretty excited," he added mischievously.

Poppy laughed. "Well come on in then. Welcome."

Thomas headed straight for the gardening magazines. It took him all of one minute to find the issues he wanted to borrow.

"What about you?" Poppy asked Aiden, "What do you like to read?"

"I'm not really sure. Thomas has asked me to build him a chicken coop that's cat, snake, and fox proof." Aiden raised his eyebrows jokingly. "Actually, I'm looking forward to collecting eggs for breakfast— there's nothing like it. Brings back a whole heap of childhood memories."

Poppy almost squealed with excitement. "I've always wanted to have chickens too. Fresh eggs for breakfast would be amazing, especially with your cooking skills. You'll be able to pimp them up no worries. That stir-fry last night was to die for. I've got the container at home. I can pop over on the weekend sometime and give it back to you."

"No rush, but it'd be great if you wanted to pop over for a cuppa."

Poppy led Aiden to the DIY collection and helped him choose a few books with building plans for different coop designs. He seemed genuinely excited and Poppy smiled as he flipped through each book commenting every so often on what was inside. After a quick browse through the DVDs, he and Thomas left Poppy to the rest of her morning.

The day brought a steady stream of customers, most of them from out of town wanting to use the Wi-Fi because they had no phone reception. Poppy felt smug that she was now local enough that people were asking her for directions and information. She was surprised by how much she'd learnt about the town in such a brief space of time. Nica had popped in a couple of times to update her on text messages from Jack, the drummer who she was now well and truly smitten with. They were planning to hook up after the band finished their set at the rodeo and Nica was so excited she'd had to tell someone. Poppy didn't have the heart to tell her that while she was looking forward to it, she equally couldn't wait for the rodeo to be over. She was worried that Rachel's expectations for the weekend were way off the mark. She'd already sent ten photos of outfits checking to see if what she was packing was 'on trend' for a rodeo. Poppy, who had basically loved op-shopping her entire adult life, had no idea what was on trend or not, so answered with a thumbs up to every image, which had eventually annoyed Rachel enough that she'd stopped texting.

Poppy waited in the truck outside the station for Rachel's train to arrive. It was getting dark and the Victorian street lights were glowing in the evening's twilight. It was almost the middle of winter and Poppy wondered how much colder it could get. She had hoped it would snow, but Gladys had broken it to her that it wasn't common in Derrin. Either way, Poppy was glad when Rachel's train finally rolled in, she was sure a thin sheet of ice had formed on the truck's windscreen.

"Hi!" Poppy called into the frosty air, her breath turning white. Rachel was making her way across the car park on kitten heals, just as Poppy had done a few days before. If felt like a lifetime ago.

"*Oh my gosh.* It took such a long time to get here. I was so bored. I lost phone reception about halfway and ate two packets of seaweed crisps and drank two coconut waters just to amuse myself." Rachel looked flabbergasted. "How am I going to live without phone reception?"

Poppy rolled her eyes. "You can use mine to contact people. It's only until Monday morning."

Rachel shook her head in mock disbelief. "The country has changed you, sis."

"Come on, let's get going. Our lift will be rocking up to my place soon and I don't want to miss the champion bronc ride and fireworks."

On the way back to Page Cottage, Poppy listened as Rachel filled her in about the truth of her and Chris's relationship. For a long time, things hadn't been as rosy as they'd seemed. Chris had been working long hours for months and they had been arguing more and more. They now had different friends and mostly different lives. Their relationship had become like a business arrangement. Rachel admitted she hadn't felt 'in love' with Chris for about a year and that it wouldn't surprise her if he was, in fact, cheating on her. As they rolled into the driveway the mood in the truck was quite somber.

"Do you still want to go?" Poppy asked Rachel who had tears in her eyes. "We can just hang here at home."

"You know what, Pops. I do. I want to have fun. I want to be like you. Throw caution to the wind.

"Like me?"

Rachel nodded. "I think that's why I was so upset about you moving out here, even though it's only for a few months. I guess I selfishly thought that you would stay in Sydney. And if you were in Sydney too, I didn't have to feel so bad for growing up there and never leaving because you were the same. My life feels so small even though the city is so big."

"Oh my gosh, Rach. I don't think your life is small at all. You have a great life. You have heaps of friends and a beautiful kid. You're kind and funny and smart."

"Thanks," Rachel sniffled, as Poppy backed the truck into the garage like a pro.

"Come on, let's get ready to go have some fun."

Once inside, it took Poppy all of fifteen minutes to throw on a pair of denim jeans and a chunky wool-knit jumper. She quickly did her makeup, brushed her long dark hair and wrapped a light grey scarf around her neck. When she emerged from the bedroom, she looked the image of country sophistication, with a touch of girl-next-door.

Rachel took longer. By the time she had finished attaching fake eyelashes and plumping her lips, Poppy had loaded up the fireplace and vacuumed the floor. Ready to leave, Poppy grabbed her handbag and called down the hall for Rachel. There was no answer.

"Sis. You almost ready? Charles has just rocked up." Poppy could see the headlights of the Land Rover in the drive.

"Hang on." Rachel's voice was muffled and Poppy wondered what she was up to.

Poppy swung her head into the guest bedroom. Sitting on the bed was Rachel grappling with a baby monitor.

"What on earth are you doing? Charles is here." Poppy wondered if her sister had lost her mind.

"Who the hell is Charles?" Rachel looked surprised with a please explain look on her face. "You've only been away for a few days and already you have men picking you up?"

"Charles is a friend. That's all, well, he may have

kissed me but that was unexpected, we're not dating, well at least I don't think we are, anyway he's picking us up." Poppy was as confused as she sounded, she couldn't blame Rachel for shaking her head.

"I'm looking forward to meeting this friend, not friend, then," Rachel cooed.

"Anyway, can you hurry up?"

At just that moment there was a knock on the front door of the cottage.

"Poppy, it's me. You ready?" Charles called from outside.

"Coming," called Poppy over her shoulder before turning her attention back to Rachel and the baby monitor. "What are you doing?"

"I'm trying to get this monitor to work, can't you see?" replied Rachel defensively.

"Why have you got a baby monitor? Ben is three," asked Poppy impatiently.

"It's not for Ben. It's for Chris," explained Rachel, as if it were obvious. "He has the house to himself this weekend. This is a prime opportunity to have someone over. I've planted a baby monitor on the kitchen bench behind the fruit bowl. If he does have company, I'll be able to hear, that's if I can get it working. It's the latest long range one." Finally, the baby monitor buzzed into action. Poppy looked on incredulously as Rachel shoved the monitor in her bag and stood up to leave. "Come on

then, you ready?" she asked as if she'd been waiting for
Poppy this whole time.

Charles stood wide-eyed in front of Poppy and Rachel.
"Wow, two stunners in one night. Lucky me!" he said,
running his hands down his chest. Poppy wasn't the
only one who noticed how good he looked in his tight
bone-coloured jeans and salmon pink shirt. She watched
on as Rachel giggled and brushed Charles' arm.

Poppy didn't want to admit it, but she felt jealous at
the way Charles was eyeing Rachel's Gucci boots and
belt. Dressed in all black, with a Pilates body to die for,
Rachel would quite possibly be the sexiest woman at the
rodeo. Poppy looked as though she'd made no effort, in
comparison.

"Charles, this is Rachel. Rachel, Charles." Poppy
felt as though her speaking was interrupting some form
of unspoken communication between the two of them.
She felt like the third wheel. Even though Charles had
kissed her only two nights ago and Rachel was married.
"Excuse me, can we go?"

"What? Yeah sure," Charles replied, peeling his eyes
from Rachel's.

As they walked through the front garden and to the
Rover, Poppy looked over to see Rachel making H O T
letters with her hands. Next door's lights were on, and

she wondered how Aiden and Thomas were spending their Friday night. Poppy secretly wished she could join them.

Walking into the rodeo, Poppy regretted arriving with Charles. All he'd done since they pulled out of her drive was talk about investments. Every second sentence had the name of someone seemingly important dropped into it. Poppy had no idea who, or what, Charles had been on about. Rachel, on the other hand, nodded her head in agreement as if she understood intimately how stock investments and crypto currency worked. Poppy knew she didn't.

Poppy watched as people of all ages filed through the entry gates. A sea of Akubra hats surrounded her. Families carried fold up chairs and picnic rugs. The smell of horses, sweat, dirt and trampled grass filled the cool evening air.

"Isn't this great?" Poppy linked arms with Rachel and jiggled up and down for warmth. "Wish I was wearing thermals though."

"It'd be warmer wearing Charles," Rachel whispered.

Poppy rolled her eyes. "May I remind you, you're married," she whispered back.

"You ladies just need a couple of drinks, to loosen

up. That's how most country girls get into the spirit of things. A few bevvies and you don't feel the cold anymore." Charles, distracted by the ping of his mobile, didn't see Poppy's forced smile. "Some business mates have just arrived, and I need to touch base."

Poppy didn't want to sound like a killjoy. "No worries," she nodded with a smile.

"Don't you two sexies go having too much fun without me," Charles winked before pecking Poppy on the cheek.

"Oh, we can't make promises like that," Rachel cooed.

There were thousands of people on the ground and Poppy could only hope that she'd be able to find Charles again before the night was over. She couldn't believe that he had just left her and Rachel. *So much for being my date.* This didn't bother Rachel at all who kept finding ways to mention how amazing Charles was.

Although the rodeo was packed, it didn't take the girls long to find Nica. She was dancing near the stage steps in gumboots and a bright yellow flip dress. The speakers boomed behind her and the stage lights flashed overhead making her hair look like wild flames. Every time the drummer picked up his beat she screamed at the top of her lungs. Poppy waved in Nica's direction as she caught her eye through the crowd. Nica signalled for them to join her.

"Hi ladies!" she buzzed.

Poppy gave Nica a hug and introduced her to Rachel. "Meet my awesome sister," she yelled into Nica's ear. Nica took Rachel's hand and mouthed something that looked like 'nice to meet you'. It was hard to tell.

"Hey, are you okay to come over to mine tomorrow?" asked Poppy.

"What?" Nica shook her head and put her hand up to her ear as if to say 'I can't hear you'.

"Come over to my place?" Poppy yelled again, "I want to put some ideas to you for fundraising and saving the community hub. What do you say to coming around just after lunch?"

"Sounds good! Hopefully, I'll be out of Jack's van by then," Nica yelled back, grinning.

As Poppy made her way over to the main arena with Rachel in tow, she could hear the crowd cheering with each horse and rider that was released from the gates. Lights flashed and ACDC's Thunder Struck blared from the speakers. The MC had the crowd laughing with every throw. 'How's that folks! Turns out the young cowboy from Byfield is slipperier than a Bunnings sausage on a Sunday and he slides off the back of the bronc in under four seconds!'

Poppy thought it quite barbaric. Rachel whooped in the air cheering on the horse. "Throw him! The bastard!" she screamed, knocking back another non-alcoholic ginger beer. The men and women in jeans, collared check shirts and cowboy hats standing around them tried to convince Rachel she was going for the wrong side, but she wouldn't have a bar of it.

Poppy had never seen Rachel this loose without a bottle of Bacardi under her belt. She was truly worried it was going to be a long night.

Less than three hours later, and what Poppy thought must have been at least a keg's worth of ginger beer drunk, Rachel was vomiting in the ladies loos and Poppy was hoping like hell that Charles would come walking by at any moment and declare he was driving them home. He did not. As it turned out, not all ginger beer is non-alcoholic and the stuff with the elephant on the label was pretty lethal. It was lucky that Poppy was still sober, although she'd wished at points she had been drunk. She'd listened to Rachel's monologue about her relationship woes nonstop for pretty much the entire night. Poppy still didn't believe that Chris was having an affair. It just didn't seem like him.

Poppy waited in the freezing cold for Rachel to surface from the toilets. When she did, she looked a mess. Her hair had bits of the hotdog they'd bought from Rose and Bob's food truck in it and toilet paper was stuck to her cheek. *How were they going to get home?* It would be impossible to get a taxi on a night as busy as this and Charles hadn't replied to any of her texts. She thought maybe they'd have a chance at walking back to the cottage, but Rachel could barely stand. Poppy was starting to seriously worry about how their night was going to wrap up when she saw Aiden and Thomas walking down from the arena stands with some mates. Aiden's smile beamed as she called over to them.

"I am so glad to see you both!" Poppy was beyond relieved. "You wouldn't be going home by any chance would you?" She knew she didn't have to explain the situation. Rachel was doing enough staggering and muttering for Aiden to get the picture.

"She's drunk," Thomas stated.

"She sure is mate," Aiden nodded. "She sure is."

"Hey Ads," one of the lads called out to Aiden, "We're heading to the bar, you coming?" Poppy recognised him as the same guy who had been chatting to Charles at the pub the other night.

"Nah Mattie, mate. We're gonna call it a night. You boys go on," Aiden yelled back.

Poppy would have dropped to her knees and begged Aiden to take them home, but thankfully, she didn't have to. Like a gentlemanly modern-day knight in shining armour, he sorted the situation by engaging a fireman lift and carrying Rachel to his ute. Which was no small feat considering she was still half conscious and protesting. Poppy followed gratefully behind and tried to decipher what Rachel was saying as she muttered something about Chris's short and curlies. Aiden carried Rachel effortlessly and by the time they'd reached his car, he hadn't even broken a sweat. "Thank you," Poppy mouthed as he bundled her sister into the backseat and handed over an old plastic shopping bag. "Just in case," he smiled nervously. The guy was risking his upholstery and Poppy hoped that they would all get home without suffering an unwanted shower.

It had taken a whole forty minutes to put Rachel to bed. She'd been adamant that the baby monitor had been deliberately quiet and that the reason she'd heard nothing was because the Gobbledok had stolen it, like it had all her potato crisps that time she went on a diet. Poppy then had to convince Rachel that the Gobbledok wasn't real, that it was pure television fiction, and that the reason the baby monitor had nothing to say was because maybe Chris didn't have any company. Every so often she heard Aiden giggle from the lounge. By the time Rachel had gone to sleep, Aiden had the fire raging and a cup of tea made for both of them.

Poppy took a warm cup from Aiden's hand and sat down on a cushion in front of the fire. She let out a long slow breath and took a sip. Her limbs relaxed as the hot, sweet taste of English breakfast ran down her throat.

"This is exactly what I need. Thank you." she yawned. Patting the floor, Poppy gestured for Aiden to come sit next to her.

"Nothing like a strong brew to finish of the night." Aiden stretched as he pulled up a cushion. "So, what did you think about your first rodeo—beside the puke?"

Poppy wrinkled her nose. "Man, I feel like it's still on my hands. I'm sure I can still smell it. I mean, it's a miracle Rachel managed to get most of it in the bag, I'm glad your ute's upholstery is safe." Poppy giggled as Aiden put his hands together in prayer and looked toward the ceiling. "The rodeo was pretty fun. I wasn't expecting so many people to be there. It's the biggest crowd I've ever seen outside of a music festival. It was great watching Thomas get into it." Poppy remembered how Thomas had been whooping in the air every time a rider was thrown off a bronc.

Aiden chuckled. "He loved seeing the riders get tossed, he's always on the horse's side. He hates they put that strap around their underbelly to make them buck and I kinda agree with him on that one. I wouldn't like someone putting a tight strap near my fishing tackle either."

"It's pretty fun watching the horses burst out of the gates. It's a bit of adrenaline rush but I think I'm with you and Thomas on the strap. Not sure I vibe with exploiting their discomfort." Poppy took another sip of her tea and stared into the glowing embers. "Will he be asleep by now?"

"Thomas? Yeah, out like a light. I'm surprised we can't hear him snoring from here." Aiden placed his hand on Poppy's shoulder. The sensation of his lingering touch was cozy and inviting. "He likes you, you know. Thomas. The way you've included him and asked him to help you with gardening has really boosted his confidence. Thank you."

Suddenly, Poppy's cheeks flushed. She turned away from Aiden's gentle gaze. "You don't need to thank me. Thomas is a fantastic gardener," she smiled softly, taking another sip of tea.

For a moment, they both sat in silence, soaking up the quiet of the night. Amber light flickered around the room and the feint smell of wood smoke lingered.

"I think this is what they mean by hygge," Poppy breathed. She looked at Aiden. His puzzled expression told her he didn't know what she was talking about. "It's a Danish thing. It describes the cultivation or unplanned occurrence of cozy moments. This moment, it's cozy," she added coyly.

"It's the most relaxed I've felt in ages." Aiden stretched his arms toward the ceiling. His shirt lifted to reveal a flash of his tanned torso and Poppy knew her cheeks blushed again. "I should probably let you get some sleep. It's got to be past midnight," he yawned. "Maybe you could tell me more about being cozy over another cup of tea sometime soon?" Aiden's eyes sparkled with sincerity.

"That'd be lovely," Poppy replied calmly, trying to contain her excitement at the thought of spending more time with Aiden. She didn't want the night to end. There was something about him that felt like a best friend, and she wondered how he was still single. Maybe it was because he worked such long hours and looked after Thomas, or maybe it was because he was waiting for 'the one', whatever the reason, the one thing Poppy knew was that she was very glad he was.

CHAPTER 14

The rest of the weekend passed without anymore ginger beer or vomit, for which both Poppy and Rachel were very grateful. Poppy had spent that Saturday morning waiting for Rachel to wake up and tiptoeing around the cottage trying to find Mr. Meow, Page Cottage's elusive cat. She'd woken, while it was still dark, to a loud crunching noise followed by a clippety-clop of what sounded for certain like claws on the cottage floorboards. The food missing from Mr. Meow's bowl told Poppy that the wayward feline had returned. But now he was no-where to be found. *Bloody cat. Where are you?* By the time Nica's bright yellow Bumblebee had turned in to the drive of Page Cottage, Poppy had given up the search—Mr. Meow had disappeared.

"BEEP. BEEP." Bumblebee's horn announced Nica's arrival.

Poppy couldn't help but laugh at the muffled swearing she heard coming from the spare room. By the time she had greeted Nica and put the kettle on, a very pale, make-up smeared Rachel stood in the hallway staring into the kitchen with eyes that squinted in the bright morning light. Her hair stuck out at all angles making her look like she'd lost a fight with a crimper. Poppy could still smell the ginger beer.

"I need a shower and orange juice." She muttered before stumbling into the bathroom.

The girls sat in the lounge in front of the fire listening to Poppy's plan to raise money for the library and community hub. They both agreed that Poppy's suggestion to use volunteer power to renew the gardens and spruce up the buildings was a great idea. But it wasn't until Poppy said the words 'spring fete' that they really got excited.

"Just think about it," Poppy said pacing around the lounge with her cup of tea and biscuit. "We can get Thomas from next door to redo the gardens and pot some cuttings to sell. We could also sell off the old books in a secondhand sale. The boys at the Men's Shed could donate some craft items and we could get the vollies to make cupcakes to sell."

"I could donate one of my artworks for a raffle and

we can sell tickets," Nica added brightly. "And I can face paint on the day."

"I could also sell the raffle tickets in Sydney," offered Rachel who held a cold towel to her head. "I can also give out flyers for the fete. If it's advertised right, you could really draw a crowd."

"Okay, so we all agree that we need to raise the money to bring the building up to standard but the thing that Council is really going to take note of is having more members. If we can argue that the hub is a vibrant part of the community then Council won't have reason to decommission it. Girls, we need to organise a membership drive. Any thoughts?"

Over the next few hours, the three of them brainstormed ideas for increasing the membership to the library and also the amount of people who used the community hub. Poppy suggested they hit the town on foot and sign up as many of the local business owners, and their families, as library members before visiting the retirement home and respite centres. Nica thought she could run life drawing classes in the garden and a nighttime nude drawing class every week—she was convinced the word 'nude' would draw a crowd and suggested Jack be their first model. Rachel proposed they invited newcomers to the community garden and start a toddler Tuesday group where children and their guardians could meet up, learn about growing food and listening to a story time. Poppy loved all the ideas and didn't see why they couldn't happen. Together, they set a date and vowed to ensure the library and community hub stayed open.

All they needed now was human power.

Come Monday morning, Poppy and Rachel were in town early for Rachel's train. Rachel had stopped obsessing over the baby monitor and had promised Poppy she would sit down and talk to Chris as soon as she got home. Poppy also made her promise that she would come back with Ben for the fete in September.

"We are going to need all the hands and help we can get," Poppy said excitedly as she gave her sister a hug. "Love you sis. I'll send you an email in a couple of days when I've got the flyer for the fete designed."

"Love you too, Pops. Thanks for always being so awesome. Apologise to your friend, Aiden, for me won't you? You know he's a really nice guy," Rachel winked.

"How would you know?" Poppy joked. "You were drunk!"

"I know these things. Call it sister's intuition," she grinned.

The rest of the morning went by without a hitch. Gladys was amicable enough. Poppy listened to her chat non-stop, about Charles this and Charles that, as she read the set-up instructions for the self-serve machine—every so often offering a 'really' or 'hmm' to appear she was paying attention. What Poppy really wanted to do was tell Gladys that her son was an absolute arse for leaving her and Rachel high and dry on Friday night, and that if it weren't for Aiden, they would never have made it home.

Poppy was glad when Gladys had finally finished shelving the returned books, and the library was quiet again. She was looking forward to weeding out the books that would be suitable for the fete's second hand book sale. Luckily, in the backroom there was already a cupboard full of deleted copies, many of them in better condition than some books on the shelves that had yellowing, stains, and torn covers. Poppy wondered who had been responsible for deleting these books and whether they had deliberately put the books of good condition into storage and the grubby books on the shelf. Surely Carmel hadn't done this, and Poppy couldn't help but wonder if Gladys had. Poppy was in the middle of moving an awkward box of books onto a trolley when Aiden came striding into the library with their returns.

"Here, let me help you with that," he said, putting the pile of books and magazines he had into the returns bin and reaching to take the box from Poppy's arms. He lifted it effortlessly. "How's your day going?" he asked.

"Pretty good. Although, I'm a bit confused by some of the management that's happened around here."

"Really, everyone says how great Carmel was."

"Yeah, but Carmel has been on sick leave for months and Gladys has been in charge. And why did Carmel leave so abruptly? Maybe she wasn't on sick leave but on stress leave. This place hasn't been managed properly for a while—long enough to not pass safety standards. The new books have been deleted and the old ratty books that should have been deleted are on the shelves. The self-serve machine isn't installed and when I got here the Wi-Fi router was gathering dust in the cupboard. The garden is in a shamble and there are procedures coming out the wazoo, but no recent reporting on expenditure or budget. And to top it off, every time I mention the budget to Gladys she brushes it off and tuts. Plus, there are other things like the door stat counter being turned off. I've just turned it back on. It's all very strange. It's almost like someone is deliberately trying to make the place unappealing."

"Hmm when you put it like that, it does sound odd. Mattie was the guy before me that did the last maintenance inspection, and he was the one who originally told Gladys that the building and grounds needed attention. Which I though interesting because when I inspected it the time before that, when Carmel was here, everything appeared up to standard."

"There's so much to do but Nica and I have a plan." As she unpacked the deleted books into a trolley, Poppy told Aiden about her ideas to save the library.

"So basically, if we can raise enough money to fix things and make the place appealing enough for people to want to come here, we should start getting more memberships. This place won't be closed down if there are enough people who want it and it's compliant."

Aiden, who seemed genuinely impressed, nodded his head in agreement. "Wow, you girls have really thought this through. If you need a hand with anything let me know. I can definitely help you while I'm not on shift."

"That'd be great. The more hands the better." Poppy knew her eagerness had nothing to do with more hands —she couldn't wait to spend more time with Aiden. "Do you think Thomas would be interested in tidying up this mess for us?" Poppy pointed to the rambling piles of weeds and old dried up plants around her.

"I'll ask him but I'm sure it'll be a yes. He doesn't stop talking about gardening."

Poppy jumped for joy. Even though, she knew she'd have to pay Thomas mostly out of her own pocket, she didn't care. *Every library deserves a chance,* she thought to herself, *and so do the people who use it.*

"So what are you going to do with this lot," asked Aiden, pointing to the previously boxed books.

"I'm going to un-delete them and put them back on the shelves."

It took Poppy all afternoon to reinstate the deleted books back into the collection. She'd spent three painstaking hours serving customers and rubbing off the permanent marker that had been used to black out the barcodes and spine labels, with eucalyptus oil. By the time she'd finished, Poppy had extremely clear sinuses and the library smelt like a koala habitat. All she needed to do now was delete most of the books on the shelves and replace them with the ones that had just been reinstated. It was a job that would take a good part of tomorrow to complete but Poppy was determined to get it done.

That afternoon, Poppy arrived back at Page Cottage to an immaculately trimmed front yard. She was amazed to see the fence for the first time. And now that the passion fruit vine had been tamed, Poppy could see the most beautiful rose bushes growing up into the mulberry tree. The yards had been mowed again and out the back the garden beds had been mended and turned over to fallow, with mulch and compost. The holes in the chicken coop had been repaired and the posts had been straightened. Poppy couldn't believe it was the same property.

"Good afternoon," called Thomas from the other side of the fence.

"Hi Thomas," Poppy beamed. "Thank you so much. The garden looks *amazing*. How did you get it done so quickly?" She was truly taken aback.

"Aiden helped me. He asked me if I want to garden at the library. I said I want to do it. I will see you there tomorrow. Thank you." Thomas waved and turned to go inside. Poppy stood astonished by his talent. She was excited to see what he could achieve with the garden at the community hub, especially if he had some helping hands to get the job done.

That night, curled up on the couch in front of the fire, Poppy fell into a deep slumber. She had been so tired that Vegemite on toast, washed down with a warming chai tea, had been the perfect dinner. She dreamt of exploring the countryside with Aiden and cooking dinner with him in his kitchen, watching funny videos with Thomas and collecting chicken eggs for breakfast. It was the nicest dream Poppy could ever remember having.

CHAPTER 15

To Poppy, it felt like the next few weeks flew by. Before she knew it, it was the end of July and her first month in Derrin had passed. And although she'd only been a part of the landscape for four short weeks, Poppy well and truly felt like she belonged in her new little community. Thomas had been at the community garden every day for the last three weeks and it was slowly coming back to life. The weeds had been completely removed and discarded into the new composting area that Tony and Clive had built on their Men's Shed days. Poppy had been ecstatic when they had agreed that something had to be done to save the community hub. All the men from the shed had banded together to renew the paths with crusher dust which had been donated from the local landscape business. The old, raised garden beds had been turned over with manure and straw collected from the local free-range organic chicken farm. And Thomas had also tamed the out-of-control nasturtiums, separated them into cuttings and repotted them in the newly built greenhouse that Aiden had relocated from Page Cottage and restored with salvaged materials. Poppy firmly believed that all the men were geniuses.

The garden had started to attract a lot of attention from locals who kept popping in to ask what was going on. Many of them believing the place had been closed for the last few months since the street sign had been removed and it had looked so overgrown. It made Poppy angry every time she had to explain to an innocent customer that they were well and truly open. The only thing that stopped her from grilling Gladys about how badly run the place had been, in Carmel's absence, was the fact that membership was now increasing and with it the borrowing statistics. And the hype was proving to be great advertising for the fete, as many of the new members kept donating books and DVDs toward the book sale. It seemed that Derrin was falling back in love with their library and this made Poppy very happy.

Nica had also been busily making mugs in between snogging Jack, teaching classes and designing flyers for the spring fete. Back in Sydney, Rachel was selling raffle tickets to win one of Nica's artworks—a beautifully detailed oil painting of a fairy wren amongst scrub from her latest exhibition. She had also put away the baby monitor and convinced Chris to go to couples counselling, for which Poppy was glad.

Everyone was busy. Everyone except for Gladys who hadn't volunteered at the library since Poppy had mentioned the need to increase memberships and raise money. She'd thought the whole idea was a waste of time and reminded Poppy of Harold and the Big Toms. In Gladys's absence, the other two volunteers, Jenny and Claris, had popped in to catch up on what had been happening. Both of them promised to make cupcakes for the fete and were genuinely excited about helping out in the community garden, now that it didn't look so frightening. Thankfully, neither of them mentioned Harold and the Big Toms.

By the beginning of August, not only was her own Page Cottage, looking picture book perfect, Poppy also thought the community hub garden looked every bit magazine worthy. And the most exciting thing was that, since the nasturtiums had been disciplined, a large storage trunk had been uncovered next to the art studio with enough pots of heritage red coloured paint to give the library and Men's Shed a once over. Both buildings were in desperate need of refreshing and Poppy couldn't wait to see them glowing.

Aiden had offered to do the painting on his off-shift days. He'd even asked Mattie if he would help, in order to get it done quicker, but he'd been busy. Poppy could not have been more grateful to Aiden and promised to make it up to him somehow. Aiden had laughed it off saying that she didn't owe him anything but, if she'd like to come out to dinner with him and Thomas on Friday night, he'd pick her up. She felt as though he really understood how important this was to her and for the first time, in a long time, Poppy felt a genuine flutter in her heart.

All she could hope for now was that when Aiden next visited the library in uniform, everything would be well on its way to being up to scratch.

That Friday night, Poppy stood in front of the bathroom mirror flustered. She couldn't get her hair right, her makeup looked over done, her contacts were itchy and she wasn't sure her outfit was right. Aiden and Thomas were taking her out for Italian, and she wanted to look sexy. Poppy hadn't been able to stop thinking about Aiden since he had started painting the exterior of the buildings that Monday. Being so close to his muscular body as it moved was pure torture. Poppy had lost count of how many times she'd been interrupted by a customer while staring longingly at his ripped torso. Arthur had asked if she was having a seizure and Mr. Jenkins had slapped closed a book in front of her face. She couldn't blame them.

Aiden was due at her door any minute and Poppy

still hadn't decided whether she should change out of her skirt and tights and into something more feminine. It was the knock at the door that made that decision for her.

"Coming," Poppy called before taking one last look in the mirror and grabbing her handbag from the kitchen. As she made her way toward the front door, she could see Aiden and Thomas' figures on the other side of the stained-glass window panel. Suddenly butterflies tangoed in Poppy's stomach. Centering herself, she took a few deep breaths before turning the doorknob.

Poppy stood breathless, caught in Aiden's spell. His gaze penetrated her.

"You look amazing," he whispered.

Poppy struggled to speak. The sight of Aiden in tight black jeans and jumper, was taking her a few seconds to recover from. She was ultra aware of the way the jumper hugged his chest. The scent of his skin, as he leant in for a hello hug, woke up her senses and sent shivers up her spine. It was earthy and sweet, like a garden. His dimples were only just visible through his trimmed beard. He looked rugged and snuggly at the same time and in that moment Poppy knew she wanted to forget dinner and wrap herself in his arms, and by the cheeky glances he'd been giving her all week, she was pretty certain Aiden felt the same way.

As he opened the car door for her, she allowed his hand to rest on the small of her back. The warmth of his palm caused her whole body to buzz and the blood to rush inside her.

The ride into town had been intense. In the dark cabin, Poppy could feel the electricity pulsing from Aiden's body the same way it had done that night they'd sat on his back verandah. She wanted to touch him—put her hand on his leg and feel him flexing with every gear change. Instead, she listened as Thomas told them about his day at respite and his plans for the community garden now that it was taking shape.

"That sounds amazing, Thomas." Poppy was in awe of his creativity.

"Thank you," he replied. "Spring is a good time to plant things, you know. The garden needs to have things you can eat in it." Thomas detailed the leafy greens and quick growing plants he thought the garden should have in it come spring. Beetroot, spinach, cabbage and mustard greens were amongst the suggestions. Poppy thought it an excellent idea and said she'd ask Nica if the art class could make identification labels.

"It'd be great if the community garden could grow enough food to host a free lunch every month for volunteers. That'd be awesome." Every time she thought about the community hub, Poppy's mind raced with excitement. The place really was going to become the heart of Derrin. Suddenly, a lump formed in Poppy's throat. She fell silent.

"What's wrong?" asked Aiden softly.

"Well, it's just that I'm not going to be here to see the benefit of all this. I'll set it up, make sure it's up to standard and I know everything will be okay. It's just that, well, I'll be gone at the end of September." Poppy stopped talking, worried that her voice would crack with the next word.

Aiden parked the ute outside the Italian restaurant on Main Street and pulled on the brake. Gently, he took her hand in his. It was warm and comforting. He looked at her with sparkly eyes and smiled knowingly. "I recon, if you want to, you should find a way to stay. I must check in on the progression of the maintenance but, as far as I can see, you're making efforts to bring things up to standard, so how about I see if we can extend the final inspection until after the fete? That'll give time for the money to be raised and for the items to be addressed."

Poppy wanted to cry. Aiden really was turning out to be a knight in shining armour, but there was still the issue of her not having any job after September. "Aiden, that would be amazing. Thank you," she said, holding back tears. "But I'm going to have to go back to the city. My contract is only until the end of September and I won't have anywhere to live once Carmel comes home."

Aiden shook his head. "I don't think Carmel is coming back. Last I heard, she was in Western Australia working in a country library over there. And Mr. Meow has been hanging out at our place since way before

Carmel moved out of the cottage. I think even he knows she's not coming back, Thomas loves him, don't you mate."

"I love him." Thomas smiled and pretended he was hugging Mr. Meow against his cheek. "He's *so* cute. When are we getting out of the car Aiden, I'm hungry."

"We can get out now, mate," Aiden laughed.

The relationship between Aiden and Thomas warmed Poppy's heart. Aiden had such a patient tenderness toward his brother, it was clear he'd do anything for him.

The Little Italian Restaurant was the cutest laneway trattoria Poppy had ever seen. Its walls were adorned with scenes of the Mediterranean, vines growing up the trellises and lanterns hanging like bunting in the open air. An eclectic collection of wooden chairs and tables gave it a homely touch. The young waiter directed them toward their table, which had homemade sourdough bread and butter waiting for them. The smell of tomatoes and garlic wafted in on the cool night air and Poppy thought she must have died and gone to Roman heaven.

The food was orgasmic and Poppy savoured every mouthful of her baked artichoke. She dipped its tender petals into a burnt butter dressing and let the saltiness wrap around her tongue with every bite. Thomas' cannelloni was also delicious, and Poppy was glad when she'd been offered a bite. The plump pasta tubes were filled with the most delicately flavoured herbed ricotta and baked to perfection. Aiden's bolognaise was rich with a heady scent of sundried tomatoes. Long thin strands of pasta danced around in the sauce as he carefully twirled it around on his fork. Poppy couldn't help but notice the way his powerful hands were gentle and deliberate with every motion.

The three of them laughed the night away and by the time they were all stuffed like fat winter chickens, Poppy was well and truly trying to find a way to stay in Derrin.

"Maybe, if Carmel doesn't come back, they'll offer me a permanent position?" she surmised enthusiastically as the ute took them back home. Aiden agreed it was possible, yet Poppy knew the only way she would be offered permanency was if the fete were a success. Word needed to get out that the community hub was the place to be and then membership growth would lead to more funding. She was grateful that Aiden was going to allow them more time until the next maintenance inspection but if the buildings didn't come up to safety standards than no amount of gardening, membership growth or new paint was going to convince Council to keep them open and the place would be shut down. For good.

The temperature had plummeted by the time they had turned onto Rose Lane. In the moonlight, the landscape looked frosted and Poppy could have sworn she saw icicles hanging off blades of grass. As soon as they parked, Thomas made his way inside to brush his teeth, leaving her standing alone with Aiden.

Poppy tried her hardest not to sound awkward. "Um, thanks for a lovely evening. It, it was great hanging out with you and Thomas."

"No worries. The pleasure was all ours. It's not often we get to share company." Aiden gestured toward Poppy's driveway before planting his hands firmly in his pockets.

"It's only a few metres and I don't want you to get a cold. I can walk myself home. It's a pretty bright night, really," smiling, Poppy tried to hide her chatting teeth.

Aiden shook his head. "Number one, a lot can happen in a few metres. And number two, I guarantee Thomas wouldn't let me hear the end of it, if I let you walk across the drive by yourself, moonlit night or not. Plus..." Poppy's heart skipped as she waited for Aiden to finish. She watched him look upward to the night sky before meeting her eyes with his own. "I'd like to walk you home," he added, coyly.

The journey across the front yard felt like both an eternity and a moment. With every step, Poppy was consumed by the presence of Aiden who walked closely beside her. Every other second their arms brushed together sending Poppy's pulse into overdrive. Their breaths, frosty in the night air, entwined creating soft misty clouds. It wasn't long before they stood awkwardly beside each other, outside the front door to Page Cottage.

"Okay, well, I guess this is goodnight," Poppy hesitated as she turned the key in the lock.

She stood motionless as Aiden took her hand in his and rested his gaze upon her. She wondered if he could feel the blood pumping through her fingers and the heat tingling her body as his thumbs stroked the tops of her fingers.

"I really like you Poppy," he whispered, bending just low enough so his nose brushed the long hair away from her ears. "You are amazing. The way you want to give to this community. I want you to stay. You've been a breath of fresh air for Thomas and I."

The sound of Aiden's voice threatened to send Poppy over the edge. It was deep and husky and penetrated every cell in her body. Her skin tingled. Poppy wasn't sure she could take anymore, a light trance encapsulated her senses as Aiden's fingertips lightly caressed her lower back.

She looked up into Aiden's brown eyes. She was grateful she didn't have to think of what to say next. Without another word, Aiden drew her near and brushed his lips against hers. They were warm and welcoming and Poppy felt herself getting lost in the moment. Aiden's tongue lightly caressed her own. Softly, it moved in and out as her lips asked for more. His hand entwined in her hair and kept her in his hold for what felt like an eternity. Poppy would have stayed kissing Aiden on the porch all night if it had not been for Thomas, who yelled, from the lounge room window, "Aiden, are you kissing?"

The two of them cracked up laughing.

"Good night Aiden," Poppy smiled as he reluctantly pulled from their embrace and walked across the front yard. "I very much want me to stay in Derrin, too," she whispered after him.

CHAPTER 16

By lunchtime Sunday, Poppy had handed a flyer for the fete into every local business. Everyone was excited to come along and some of the café owners even offered to donate baked goods to sell at the cupcake stand. The local hardware owners had also offered to give Thomas a whole heap of seedlings they'd propagated in their greenhouses over the winter to plant in the community garden. As far as drumming up support for the fete, the weekend was an absolute success. And although it had been busy, Poppy had even found time to visit Nica's exhibition. She was surprised at how long it had been since they'd shared a chat and was eager to tell Nica all about her and Aiden.

"Hiya stranger." Nica's bubbly voice rang out through the exhibition space.

Poppy stood wide-eyed in front of the beautiful

paintings that adorned the white gallery walls. Large images of wrens, bird nests and native flowers came to life and lifted from the canvasses.

"Nica, your work is fantastic. You are so talented," beamed Poppy. "And look at all those red dots!"

"Thanks mate," Nica glowed. "Yeah, I've sold a lot."

Poppy walked up close to the paintings, taking in every bit of fine detail. She read each label carefully and then turned her attention to a white wall mounted card that displayed information about Nica's artistic practice. The description of Nica's love for the environment and local natural heritage was inspiring, but it was the last sentence that brought tears to Poppy's eyes. *All proceeds from this exhibition will be donated to reviving the buildings and community garden in the Library's Community Hub.*

"There's quite a bit raised," said Nica sheepishly, "about five thousand dollars so far and still room for more."

Poppy gave her friend a big hug. Tears trickled down her face. She couldn't believe how it was all coming together. This meant that they could start to action the points on the maintenance report straight away, starting with the fire and hazard safety items. "Nica, you are truly amazing!"

"Thanks," blushed Nica. "I've also decided to use some of my savings to buy the materials needed to start up the different art classes I was talking about." Nica took a deep breath. "I'll have more time now that I'm single again."

"Oh Nica, I'm so sorry. What happened?"

"Jack decided he didn't want to be tied down. He left to go on tour last week. It's why I've been keeping to myself, just processing it all and trying to work out what the next year holds for me."

"I'm sorry to hear it didn't work out."

"Ah don't be, it's probably for the best. Plus, I've been thinking about moving. I've been in Derrin my whole life and I'm itching to do something different, see a bit of the world. I've always wanted to live in England. I have family in Cornwall. I've applied for an artist residency at the Tate gallery. It's a long shot but you've got to be in it to win it, don't you? Plus, my tarot cards said change is coming."

Overwhelmed by how generous Nica was being, Poppy sniffled and shook her head. Gifting so much money toward saving the community centre, even though she wasn't planning on staying, was a big deal. "I'd miss you if you went but it would give me an excuse to come over and visit you."

"I'm just going to wait and see what happens. I find out about the residency, about the same time as the fete."

"I hope you get it," Poppy said wiping another tear from underneath her glasses. "Man, September is really going to be a crazy month. And it's almost here."

"I know," replied Nica, as she placed a red sold sticker next to a painting of Australian native flowers. "I can't believe it either. I just really need a change of scenery. I've been in this town for what feels like forever and I haven't really lived. I need an adventure. Plus, people keep telling me I should take my art more seriously, do it full time, and I reckon it's about time I did."

"Well, I'm sorry things didn't work out between you and Jack," Poppy bit her lip. "I'll miss you but I think travelling and seeing another part of the world will be amazing and think about all that inspiration for your paintings; and all the men with sexy accents," Poppy grinned. She was glad to see Nica giggle. "You really are talented. I mean, just look at the detail in your paintings, the way you depict the softness of bird feathers and the cheekiness in their eyes, it's really stunning."

"Thanks, mate." A rosy hue graced Nica's cheeks. Poppy knew she would miss her friends' bright sunny energy. "Anyway, enough about me. Tell me all about you. How did it go with Charles?"

"Charles has ghosted me ever since the rodeo. I haven't heard from him at all." Poppy slumped into the chair next to the gallery sales counter. "He's an interesting guy, but he just talks about himself all the time. I mean, he never really attempted to find out about me. And then on the night of the rodeo he just left us and I didn't hear an apology or anything from him at all! Seriously, if it hadn't been for Aiden, I don't know what I would've done. Rachel was blind—well, you saw her the next day."

Nica shook her head. "Guys these days. Who do they think they are, God's gift or something? Looks like neither of us are having much luck in that department."

"Well…" grinned Poppy. Just as she heard the gallery door swing open behind her, Nica's unexpected cough let her know not to speak any further. She turned around to see who had entered.

"Poppy," Charles Batsy, stood in the doorway looking suave in a light grey suit and polished tanned shoes. His blonde hair slicked back against his head. Poppy watched the way he fidgeted with the button on his jacket. "It's nice to see you."

"Hello Charles, fancy seeing you here," Poppy replied far too quickly. "I'm just chatting to Nica. Aren't her paintings amazing?"

"They are indeed," nodded Charles. "Look I'm glad I've run into you. I saw you in here and I've been meaning to apologise for the rodeo. I was a horrible date. I got caught up with chatting to business mates, networking, you know, and completely forgot about the time and I didn't get your texts until the next morning. Mattie kept bringing out rounds of drinks. He'd just come into his inheritance and was celebrating by shouting everyone."

Poppy raised her eyebrows. "I didn't know you and Mattie were business mates."

"We are now. He's invested in a local project I've got going on. Anyway," Charles dismissed, "the point is, I should have called a cab for you and Rachel, and I didn't. It was not very gentlemanly, and I'd like to make it up to you, if I can?"

Poppy tapped her toe on the floor, hesitantly. She was acutely aware that Nica stood by listening to every word and probably hoping she would tell Charles to 'stick it' "Look, Charles..."

"I know I was an idiot, Poppy," Charles interrupted. Without invitation, he stepped closer and lowered his voice. "It really was an important business opportunity. Think about it and if you'd like to go out, you know my number. I promise, I'll reply this time." Charles didn't wait for an answer. Instead, he winked and turned on his heels. Before Poppy had time to open her mouth, he was strutting out the door, leaving as quickly as he came, in an air of self-importance.

"Why does he have to pop back up now?" Poppy sighed with frustration. "Just after Aiden kissed me too."

"Say what?!" Nica's jaw dropped. Her expression was priceless.

"A fly might land in there," Poppy joked.

"I'm sorry, did you just say Aiden kissed you?"

"Yeah. He did. Friday night. And it was bloody brilliant," said Poppy, dreamily.

"Tell me everything." Nica pulled over another chair and sat next to Poppy. She rested her chin in her hands and waited.

"Well, he and Thomas took me out for Italian. The conversation flowed, we chatted about music, food, family and trips we'd like to take. Thomas chatted about gardening. It was really lovely. He drove me back to mine and walked me to my door, and then he kissed me. It was slow and sexy and it woke up parts of me that have been numb for ages. I cannot remember the last time I was kissed like that. He, he's amazing." Nica's giggle woke Poppy up from her delicious memory.

"You should see the look on your face!" Nica jested, "You're in love. And more importantly, my tarot cards were right."

Poppy laughed. "We're far off being a couple. He just kissed me, nothing else."

"It's a start and seriously, I was starting to think Aiden never wanted another relationship again. Not after he was cheated on by his fiancé," Nica said as she got up to straighten a painting.

"Hang on, what? He didn't tell me he used to be engaged."

"Yeah, a few years back now. She really hurt him, too. They were engaged for a couple of years. She was working in the city and coming back on weekends. One weekend she just never came back. He found out later that she'd moved in with a guy she worked with. She broke off their engagement in one phone call. Aiden's been single ever since. But he's been different since you've come to town, though. He seems lighter. He doesn't look like he carries the weight of the world on his shoulders anymore."

"Have you known Aiden for long?" Poppy asked.

Nica nodded. "We went to high school together so I guess he's always been in the background. We had mutual friends, you know. I bet he's happy you came here."

Poppy smiled. "I'm pretty happy I came here, too. To think the spring fete is only a few weeks away. Aiden and Thomas have done so much to help. And the fresh paint on the buildings looks amazing. Really brightens the place up. Now, with the money you've raised, we'll be able to sort the fire and safety items this week. And maybe, if you don't mind, we can buy some new books and DVDs. Now that memberships are slowly increasing, we'll need more items."

"Sounds good," Nica said as she jumped up on a stool and straightened one of the hanging wires. "I'll start advertising my new life drawing classes for next week, we can start by drawing the structures in the garden and our own hands and feet until I find someone who will nude model, you wouldn't ask Aiden would you?" Nica winked.

"Hey, hey, friend. A step too far." Poppy raised her hand in mock seriousness.

"Drats," Nica pouted, pretending to be disappointed, "I know for sure a man-*not*-in-uniform would definitely draw a crowd, especially one as sexy as Aiden."

"The only person who I want to see Aiden naked is me."

Nica and Poppy sat giggling for another half an hour chatting about men and swapping sex stories. The two of them could have chatted all afternoon but Poppy wanted to get back to the cottage and prepare for the week ahead. There was so much to do and now that they had the money to do it, she would have to get onto organising the fete, repairs to the library and the new fire safety equipment as soon as possible.

CHAPTER 17

The next two weeks passed by lightning fast. Nica had started her life drawing classes and was attracting a crowd of ten or more people to each session. They spent their time in the garden drawing each other, as well as bugs and birds, twigs, and lines of the surrounding buildings. Poppy was impressed by the talent that the group had, and she and Nica had spent many hours discussing the Art Studio's end of year exhibition. It was Nica's brilliant idea to bring the exhibition date forward and hold an open-air show in the community hub grounds at the same time as the fete. Poppy agreed that it would be the perfect opportunity to draw a crowd and showcase local talent. The improvements at the hub were causing quite a stir in town, with people coming in every day to ask about the different programs on offer. Clive had signed up seven new members to the Men's

Shed, and the Gardening Club, as Thomas now called it, had a whopping twenty enthusiastic helpers.

Poppy hadn't seen much of Aiden since they'd kissed that Friday night. Between her being at the library and his being at work, they'd been like ships in the night only catching brief glances and small hellos when Aiden dropped Thomas off at the community garden. Poppy wondered if Aiden was having second thoughts about her. She had found it hard to believe that someone as sexy and amazing as Aiden would be interested in her and she was starting to think that maybe it was too good to be true. Nica had assured her that Aiden was probably just taking things slow, that maybe he didn't want to get involved too quickly and get hurt again. The only thing that stopped Poppy from sending Aiden a gazillion text messages and falling into a self-wallowing pit of despair was her never-ending to do list.

Every day there was a hype of activity and slowly the hub was becoming what Poppy had envisaged it to be, the heart of the community. The library had increased its visitor-ship by fifty percent and volunteers Jenny and Claris, who Poppy found out were both retired primary school teachers, had started running story-time in the garden. Gladys still hadn't been into the library since Poppy had asked her about the budget. Charles, however, had been in almost every day enquiring about business and asking questions about the fire and maintenance report. It seemed that Poppy's effort to ignore his offers to make up for the rodeo debacle was only making him more eager to win her over.

"Good morning beautiful," he'd said one morning as he swanned on in through the library carrying two takeaway coffees. Poppy hoped he wasn't planning on staying.

"Charles, what a surprise. I wasn't expecting to see you since you were in here only yesterday, and the day before that. What brings you back?"

"Just wanted to come in and see how your day is going." He passed over a coffee.

"Thanks." Not wanting to be rude, Poppy took the cup from Charles' hand. "It's only just gone 9:00 AM, though. I've barely opened."

"True. So, what have you got on for today?" Charles asked, running his finger along the spines of new romantic fiction that had just been shelved by Claris.

"I've got some trades people coming in to make repairs to the art studio and later this afternoon the company who maintains the fire and safety equipment is coming to action the outstanding items flagged in the last report. The next inspection is due the Monday after the spring fete, so everything has to be in order by then."

"In order, hey? What do you mean?" Charles perked up.

"Oh, it's no big deal. Well, not now. But when I got here the library and community hub buildings didn't pass the fire and safety inspection. Council said that they would be decommissioned if they weren't up to standard. Aiden's doing the next inspection, just after the fete, but Nica has sold so many paintings and raised heaps of money that we have been able to action the bits that need doing now." Poppy took a sip of her drink as she explained the situation. Charles' expression had turned very serious and she could tell he listened intently. "I have to write a report after the next inspection and provide evidence to the Council that the community hub is still a viable investment. It shouldn't be a problem—our new memberships are going crazy and the place is always busy. Steve and Donald, over at the Men's Shed, have been collecting signatures and feedback from customers who love this place. It's all going into the report."

"Sounds like you've got it all sorted. Are you sure it's going to pass the fire and safety inspection, though? I mean, from what I heard the place was pretty run down."

"It was. Well structurally everything was mostly okay, apart from the art studio, but funding wasn't being spent in the right areas and things had been left by the wayside. But I'm pretty confident we've almost sorted it. I'm going to get Aiden to come in just before the fete to give it an informal once over, so I know without doubt everything's been done. Council won't want to decommission this place if it meets standards and is being used."

"Why do you care so much if they decommission it? You'll be back in the city. Maybe there are better uses for the land?" Poppy couldn't believe what Charles was saying. How could he be so uncaring about the place she'd been pouring her heart and soul into for the last month and a half?

"Like what better uses for the land? This place is important to heaps of people and me. Plus, I'm hoping to stay," Poppy said feeling miffed at Charles' attitude.

"Stay?" Charles eyebrows shot toward the ceiling. He looked genuinely surprised. "Here? But there's literally *nothing* to do in this town."

"That's not true at all," Poppy felt herself getting defensive. She rubbed her lotus tattoo and took a deep breath. She wondered why she felt the need to defend the community hub against Charles, anyway. "Derrin is awesome and I've made friends here. I feel a part of something," she added earnestly.

Charles opened his mouth to protest, but had no time for a rebuttal. Poppy's phone began ringing, and she was grateful for the interruption. "Sorry, Charles, I've got to take this. It's business. You understand." Looking a bit stunned, Charles nodded his head and turned toward one of Nica's paintings.

"Hi Rachel," Poppy was glad to hear her sister's

voice. Although, she'd texted her to tell her about her steamy kiss with Aiden, it had been ages since she'd spoken to Rachel and was keen to hear how things were going back in the city.

"Oh my God, sis! You are never going to believe it," Rachel squealed.

"What? Tell me."

"I've sold ALL the raffle tickets for Nica's painting —the entire book gone. Plus, Chris has promised he's going to cut back on work. He and I have been doing the couple's counselling thing, and it's really working. We haven't argued in over two weeks and we've had sex almost every day. You've totally got to try Tantra. It's amazing. Last night, Chris did something with my..."

"Whoa! Okay. Let me stop you there. Two seconds." Poppy held her phone against her stomach and smiled at Charles who seemed to have gotten bored with the painting and was now waiting for her to finish the call. He put his hand up as a sign he'd gotten the message. "Sorry, Charles. This is going to take longer than I thought. Thanks for the latte though, I really appreciate it."

"All good," he mouthed. "I'll catch you later."

Poppy turned her attention back to Rachel who was still talking on the other end of the phone, "and then he did this twisty thing. We are totally out of honey now."

Poppy cringed. She didn't want to imagine what Rachel and Chris had been doing with honey.

"So what about you? How'd it go with Aiden after your steamy kiss?"

"I haven't really seen much of him. I'm going to pop around there this afternoon though. I have some money to give to Thomas. I'm not entirely sure Aiden likes me in that way now."

Poppy heard Rachel sigh down the phone. "Pops. You have to start taking risks. You can't wait for Aiden to make the first—well, second move—he might be just as nervous as you are. I've got to go. I promised Chris I'd send him a nudie pic and I have to go shave before I pick Ben up from daycare."

"I'm not going to ask for the details," Poppy laughed, glad Rachel was happy again. Poppy knew she was right. If she wanted things to progress with Aiden, she'd have to tell him how she felt. The fete was only a couple of weeks away and her contract would end soon.

That afternoon, Poppy could feel a change in the air. The grass smelt different, the sunset lingered on the horizon and the birds had started to sing in a way that let the world know spring was coming. There was a renewal underfoot, a sense of possibilities, and with it, an excitement. Poppy couldn't wait to tell Aiden about the accomplishments at the community hub and how awesome Thomas had the garden looking in preparation for planting out seedlings this coming week.

Standing in front of the bathroom mirror, Poppy blinked her contacts into place and gave herself the once over. She was always amazed to see how different she looked without her glasses. *Definitely not girl next door now.* Her tight, dark blue skinny leg jeans hugged her slender figure and the pink cotton flannelette shirt she'd tied at the waist accentuated her curves. She'd rolled her shirtsleeves up just high enough to show her tattoo and untied her bun to let her long brown locks fall naturally down her back. She felt sexy and a new version of herself. Dabbing a touch of gloss to her lips, a renewed sense of confidence washed over her. *If this doesn't send Aiden crazy, I don't know what will.* She gave herself a 'you got this wink' in the mirror, before grabbing the envelope with the money she owed Thomas and heading out the house.

Standing at Aiden's front door, she rubbed her tattoo and reminded herself to breathe. Butterflies danced in her stomach and her heart fluttered. *This is ridiculous, Poppy. Pull yourself together. He's just a man, there's nothing to be afraid of!*

Just then the door burst open. Aiden stood before her. His ripped body almost filled the doorway. Clad only in a towel, water droplets glistened on his skin. His muscles quivered in the cool air. Poppy noticed the goose bumps forming across his tanned torso and his nipples tighten in the breeze. His chest rose and fell deeply. Poppy's breath quickened.

"Hi," she whispered.

"Hi," he whispered back. "It's good to see you. I was going to pop over after my shower, but I'm glad you're here." Aiden's dark brown eyes sparkled in a way that immediately set Poppy at ease. "I'm so sorry I haven't been able to get over to the community hub or check in to see how you were in person," he continued earnestly. "I know the phone doesn't always cut it. This lot of shifts has been hectic..."

Poppy waited for Aiden to finish his sentence. He didn't. Instead, he leaned back against the doorframe with his hands behind his head. Poppy watched the way his biceps flexed. They were about the same size as her thighs and threatened to send her over the edge. He grinned as if he knew the anguish, he caused her.

"What?" Poppy asked nervously.

"You. You look amazing." Aiden's gaze traced Poppy's legs and wandered over her hips before landing on her breasts. She felt her nipples harden under his gaze. The envelope for Thomas shook in her hands.

"So do you," she replied, feeling like she might combust at any moment.

"Listen, I have to get to work but how about I come around to the library tomorrow and bring lunch? We can catch up properly. I've got next week off, leading up to the fete, so I'll be able to help you in whatever way you need."

Poppy knew exactly how Aiden could help her, and it had nothing to do with the community hub. Feeling overwhelmed with aching in places that hadn't ached for a long time, Poppy nodded. "Sure, um, yeah, yep, that'd, that'd be great." Turning to leave before she feinted from an overload of sexual energy, she handed the envelope to Aiden. "It's Thomas' payment for the work at the community garden so far. Also, I want to ask Thomas if he'd like to stay on permanently as head gardener—that's if the Council agrees not to decommission the place and we get funding."

Aiden nodded. "Ask him after the fete once you've heard formally from the Council. I don't want to get his hopes up." Before Poppy had time to say that she was sure everything would be okay, Aiden had leant down and silenced her lips with his own. He pulled her in close, pressing his hips against hers. The warmth sent blood rushing to every inch of her body. Suddenly her clothes felt veil thin against her sensitive skin. Aiden's hardness left Poppy with no doubt that he felt the same way about her. "See you tomorrow," he whispered, his breath warm against her ear.

CHAPTER 18

The next day, Poppy found herself in the community garden listening to Thomas explain his plans for planting out the seedlings he'd cultivated in the greenhouse over winter. He had everything from tomatoes, squash, zucchinis, beans, cucumbers, brassicas and even strawberries. During the clean up, Thomas had found a few citrus trees, two blueberry bushes and an apple tree, which excited everyone.

"So, Poppy, the tomatoes can go here." Thomas pointed to a trellis he'd made from bailing twine and twigs. "The cucumbers need sun and water so they can go over there, near the shed. The squash will grow big so it can go near the front gate, next to the zucchinis and beans can grow up the fence. The strawberries can go underneath the blueberries and apple and the nasturtiums can stay under the tomatoes. Oh, and the cutting lettuces and kale can go near the tomatoes too."

"Wow! Thomas, this is amazing! Come next year this place will produce enough food for a feast." Poppy looked around amazed.

"Yes, we will!" Thomas cheered with a smile so big it warmed Poppy's heart.

"What are we all cheering about?" asked a familiar voice.

"Charles! What are you doing here?" Poppy was surprised to see him. She thought he would have given up by now but there he stood, dressed in another immaculate suit with a clipboard under his arm.

"I've just come to say hello. Thought I'd take a proper look around at all the hard work you've all put it."

"We have worked hard," piped up Thomas, whose smile had suddenly been replaced with a deadpan stare. "I must go back to work now, Poppy. I've got things to do."

"No worries Thomas, I'll catch you later." Poppy watched Thomas go back to sorting out his seedlings. She couldn't help but notice his sudden change in demeanour. Charles, who seemed completely oblivious, continued to go on about how he thought that fixing up the buildings was a waste of time.

"It's nice that you want to pretty things up, Poppy, but is it really going to make any difference?" Charles shrugged. "I mean, they're just a bunch of old buildings. Surely the library and community groups would be better off somewhere newer."

Poppy couldn't believe the nerve of the guy. Did he really think she cared so little about what happened to the community hub that he could talk so openly about his negative opinions in front of her?

She was just about to say something when Aiden, dressed in his Paris-blue uniform with lapels on his shoulder, walked through the front gate carrying three cardboard takeaway containers. Thomas perked up as soon as he saw him.

"Hi mate," Aiden waved.

"Hi Aiden," Thomas called out.

Poppy felt her heart leap. "Hiya," she beamed momentarily, forgetting that Charles stood beside her.

"Quinoa salad with roast veg, herbs and feta," Aiden said as he passed her the lunch container and eyed Charles. "There's one for Thomas too."

"Well, well. If it isn't Aiden Baxter." Charles squared his shoulders and extended his hand.

"Charles Batsy. I heard you were in town. All suited up, mate." Aiden returned the handshake. "Looking all very official. What are you here for?"

"You know, Aiden, this and that. I've got some business around here at the moment." Poppy watched the way the two men stood, arms crossed and rigid, pretending to be friendly.

"You two know each other?" she asked.

"High school," Charles answered. "Although I was more mates with Mattie. He's in the fire department now, yeah? You two are on the same shift crew?"

Aiden nodded. "That's right. Mattie's been in the job longer than me, though. So, what is it you're here for, Charles?"

Poppy wondered the same thing. She hadn't invited Charles and she couldn't help but wonder if he was just there to pass the time until his next business meeting.

Charles smiled directly at Aiden. "I'm here to visit Poppy, say hello, see how her day's going. We have so much in common, both of us being from the city and all. We were just about to organise a catch up drink..." Poppy widened her eyes and opened her mouth to speak, but Charles interrupted again. "I'll text you later Poppy. Enjoy your lunch."

Aiden turned to Poppy as soon as Charles was out of earshot. "Is there something I should know about you two?"

"Oh my gosh, no. Absolutely not. No way. Charles has been hanging around a lot lately, but I haven't given him any reason to."

Aiden nodded his head. Lightness returned to his face. "Yeah, the guy always has been a jerk. He left town years ago. I'd like to know why he's hanging around now."

"Me too, but really, it's got nothing to do with me,"

Poppy replied earnestly, shaking her head. Hoping that their conversation would turn away from all things Charles Baxter, she returned to her lunch. Sharing a conversation with Thomas and Aiden was the highlight of her day. She felt so at ease with them. She loved listening to Thomas chat constantly about gardening, just as much as she loved laughing at Aiden's jokes. There was something about the three of them together that brought her joy.

"Tell Poppy what we are getting after the fete," Aiden said cheekily.

Thomas's eyes lit up. He grinned from ear to ear. "Chickens!"

Poppy squealed so high; salad almost came out of her mouth. Aiden and Thomas cracked up laughing and Poppy wondered how it was that they felt so much like family.

CHAPTER 19

Before Poppy knew it, it was the week before the fete. There was still so much to do. She was grateful to Aiden and Thomas for being on hand to help and Nica had the volunteers organised in such a militant style, Gladys would have been impressed. For someone who used to be so proactive about running the library, Poppy still did not know why she hadn't seen her since July. Jen and Claris had commented briefly that Gladys and Derek had been seen out and about in town with Charles, Mattie Boyle, and some men who looked like tradies. Poppy could only assume that it all had to do with this 'business' Charles kept mentioning he had. It was no concern of hers though.

That Monday, the members and volunteers of the community hub met in the garden. Everyone was fuelled by hot tea and ready to get started.

"So," Poppy continued, "Donald and Steve, if you could help Nica. She has the plan for installing the garden sculptures. Tony and Clive, you are going to position the Harold 'Big Tom' memorial seat, yes?" Both men nodded seriously. "Jenny and Claris, you are sourcing all the items we will need for the tea and cupcake station on the day?" Jenny nodded and mentioned that she and Claris had carefully combed the books in the library's cooking section and had found a cupcake recipe that was sure to sell hundreds. "Thomas, you're in charge of putting the plant tags with the right plants..." Thomas made a fist pump he was so excited. "And Aiden, you're finishing the painting on the repaired sections of the art studio. That just leaves me who will be running the library and starting on the end of month report for the Council. Oh, and Rachel and Ben will arrive on Saturday morning to help with the big day. One more thing, the wonderful Nica has organised for Bob and Rose, from down the pub, to put on a sausage sizzle during the day." The group cheered. Poppy was amazed by how charged and ready to go everyone was. It had never been this easy to rally the troops together in her old job, and she was grateful to every single one of them for their passion and enthusiasm. Just as everyone was heading off to their tasks, Nica came running up to Poppy.

"Pops! Pops! Pops! Poppy!" she bounced, her red curls bobbing up and down like little springs.

"What! What! What! What!" Poppy laughed.

"I've been shortlisted!"

"No?!" Poppy held her hands over her open mouth.

"Yep! Shortlisted. I'm in the running for the residency in Cornwall. I could be moving to England." Both girls pranced and giggled on the spot. "Okay, okay," Nica said, calming down. "Don't tell anyone. Not until I actually get in. There's still a chance that I might not. But shortlisted!" Poppy happy danced with Nica one last time before heading back into the library. *This week*, she thought as she glanced back toward the garden, *is going to be epic.*

And epic it was. Poppy was proud of the way everyone worked together. By the time Friday morning rocked around, she was happily knackered. Claris and Jen had single-handedly baked and iced two hundred cupcakes ready for the cake stall. The gents from the Men's Shed had installed the bespoke garden sculptures, made by Nica's respite group pottery club, throughout the grounds, and Harold's memorial seat in the new tomato patch. "He would have wanted it this way, being the joker he was," they'd answered when Poppy questioned its positioning. She wasn't sure if having the seat's final resting place, exactly where Harold had died, would be seen as inauspicious.

Thomas had carefully placed an identification label next to each planted seedling. Poppy loved the neat little rows he'd formed in some beds and the wild everything-in look he'd created in others. Little green leaves popped up everywhere. The community garden had come alive. She was also grateful that Aiden had straightened all the retaining walls around the raised beds and made sure the paths were smooth and swept. He'd finished painting the art studio and touched up missed bits on the outside of the library. Together, he and Thomas had made a scarecrow out of old cowboy clothing and everyone admired what a great job they'd done, Arthur, returning books one day, remarked that it looked like Gladys. Charles had only popped in twice to get updates on their progress. Whilst Poppy wasn't interested in dating Charles, she thought it kind of him to check in and see how they were going with everything, even if he never actually offered to lend a hand.

The last couple of days had been so busy; Poppy had barely had time to connect with Aiden, and she was glad to finally have a moment of privacy. Together, they sat on the back steps of Page Cottage sharing a soda water and watching the last of the day's light fade. After a week of lustful gazes and sneaky touches, they were finally alone.

"I've been itching to have some alone time with you all week," whispered Aiden. Poppy felt her knees tremble as he brushed her hair with his fingers. "The eve of the big day, hey? How do you feel?"

"Um, I'm fine, a, a bit nervous." Poppy found it

hard to concentrate. Her mind was a jumble. "Everything's sorted. Nica's paintings raised heaps of money already, so the fete is just a booster now, plus we'll be able to pay Thomas the rest of what he's owed. I just hope everything's good enough to pass the inspection next week." Poppy rubbed her lotus tattoo and took a deep breath.

She was conscious of the way Aiden watched her. "Don't worry about the inspection," he said softly. "I looked at everything yesterday, after I finished the last of the painting off, and it all looks good. I have to do the inspection formally, but it will be fine."

In that moment Poppy felt a wave of gratitude wash over her. She couldn't believe it was the beginning of September and in four short weeks her contract would be up. Carmel hadn't been in contact with the library in any way so Poppy wasn't sure she could be guaranteed of staying on, even if the place was saved. The thought of leaving broke her heart.

"What's up," asked Aiden.

Poppy didn't want to answer in case her emotions betrayed her. "Well," she swallowed hard. "It's just that, I'm really excited to save the library and the community hub, but I'm still not guaranteed that Carmel won't come back. I haven't been offered an extension on my contract. If it isn't renewed, then I'll have no job and nowhere to live," Poppy sighed.

"You can come live with us," smiled Aiden coyly.

"Mr. Meow has already made our lounge room his home."

"Mr. Meow! That dirty little minx," Poppy laughed.

"He's probably watching that funniest home videos animal show with Thomas, right now."

Poppy rolled her eyes in disbelief.

"Seriously. He spreads out on the carpet like he's paying the mortgage." Aiden's chuckle brought a smile to her face. She loved hearing him laugh. It made her giggle. "Oh Aiden, I'm..."

Poppy didn't have time to finish telling Aiden she was happy he and Thomas had walked into her life. The sensation of Aiden's fingers moving lightly over the small of her back lulled her into a brief moment of amnesia. She struggled to string words together. Her skin tingled. Shivers pulsed through her body, it ached with every stroke. Her breath quickened as he gently pulled her into his lap. Before Poppy could gather her senses, Aiden's lips, warm and soft, caressed her neck and brushed against her ear. The heat of his breath threatened to send her over the edge. Without warning, in one smooth move, Aiden swooped Poppy into his arms and stood to his feet. In a few quick steps, he had her pressed against the backdoor of Page Cottage. Poppy's breath caught in the back of her throat. Aiden's muscles, taut and tanned, brushed against her sides. His hips rocked against her pelvis.

Poppy thought she might lose her mind. Her

heartbeat quickened as Aiden's pecs brushed against her breasts. Grasping his back with one hand she groaned in ecstasy. Desperate to get him inside, Poppy fumbled with the latch. Her legs tightened around his torso. She gasped as his hands tangled into her hair and his tongue ran along her collarbone. Poppy was thankful she wasn't wearing glasses. They'd well and truly be foggy by now. She wanted Aiden more than she'd ever wanted anyone. His body. His smell. His voice. His touch. He drove her wild. She wanted him to devour every inch of her.

"Damn, you drive me wild, Poppy," he growled as he unbuttoned the top of her blouse, his breath warm against her nipples. "Ever since the day with the ladder, I've wanted you. You don't know how much the sight of you drives me crazy. Your body. Your laugh. Your smile. Your kindness. I lose it when I'm around you. You're the sexiest, smartest, loveliest woman on the planet. Are you crying?" For a second, Aiden looked genuinely shocked.

Poppy giggled. "No, it's my damn contacts," she said, wiping her eye. "I'm still getting used to them. Now, what was that about me being lovely?" she whispered as she bit his ear.

"That feels... oh man," he groaned.

"I want you, Aiden. I want you now."

Poppy woke the next morning at dawn, to the smell of warm toast and fried eggs. The sound of the pan sizzling and the jug bubbling made her smile. As if he knew she was awake, Aiden, clad only in a towel around his waist, walked in on cue with a hot cup of earl grey and a freshly made hot water bottle.

"Well, this is a nice way to wake up in the morning," Poppy winked. "Thank you."

Aiden placed the hot water bottle underneath the covers and the tea on the bedside table. "Don't get up, gorgeous," he said. "The house isn't warm enough yet."

"What's the time?" asked Poppy, slightly worried that it was later than she'd expected.

"It's just coming up to six-thirty. You've got heaps of time. When did you tell Nica you'd meet her?" Aiden asked.

"Eight. We want to get there early to set up the open-air exhibition and hang some bunting. Jen and Claris will be there about nine to set up the cake stall and Tony will be there around nine-thirty with the rest of the shed crew."

"And what about Rose and Bob? Are they still doing the food?" Aiden called out as he made his way back to the kitchen. Poppy could hear the scraping of the egg flip against the pan. Her stomach rumbled. Having had something sexier than food for dinner last night, she didn't realise how hungry she'd been.

"The sausage-sizzle, yep. They'll start that around

eleven. Nica will be manning the exhibition with some volunteer helpers from her respite group and I'll be walking around handing out forms for library memberships."

"Thomas is looking forward to showing people around the garden. He mentioned it this morning, when I popped over to see if everything was okay. We'll get there around ten. You wouldn't believe who was curled up in bed with Thomas when I went over?"

"No way?"

"Yep," Aiden nodded, "Mr. Meow. I now know why there's always tiny black fur in the washing machine after Thomas washes his sheets."

"I think he might be your cat now," chuckled Poppy.

"I'm not really a cat person, but I think you might be right. Hey, what time are Rachel and Ben getting here?"

"I think their train gets in around nine-ish. They are going to stay here tonight and go back tomorrow."

Aiden came walking into the bedroom carrying in two plates of eggs on toast. The smell of the warm yolks covered in melting butter and salt and pepper made Poppy's mouth salivate. "Well, I look forward to enjoying this morning with you then, before the madness starts," he winked.

Poppy stood silently, in the community hub garden, waiting for Nica to arrive. The beds were covered in early morning dew and some paths had a light frost on them. Poppy's heart swelled with pride at the hard work everyone had put in to make it happen. The place had a new energy about it and glistened with potential. Poppy could have stood there all day in appreciation, if it weren't for Nica, who came bustling cheerily through the front gates carrying a bag of bunting under one arm and the painting for the raffle under the other. In her bright blue polka dot dress and cowgirl boots, she was dressed for a party and Poppy, who had chucked on jeans and a flannelette shirt to fit in, felt a bit plain in comparison.

"Hiya!" Nica waved. "It's a beautiful day for a fete," she beamed.

Poppy agreed it was splendid. The sky sparkled clear blue, and the sun glistened. They couldn't have asked for more brilliant weather.

Over the next half hour, Poppy and Nica nutted out the perfect location for each easel and plinth in the open-air exhibition. They decided the artworks were best highlighted if they were positioned around the outside of the garden. That way, people could easily walk up to view them. Poppy was impressed by the talent Derrin had. Some works were abstract and others were more realistic. Poppy's favourite clay sculpture was titled Mr. Jenkins. With its open mouth, long drawn face and bulging eyes, it somewhat resembled Edvard Munch's 'The Scream'. The works from participants of Nica's new life drawing classes rested in the easels, and Poppy loved the juxtaposition of having the pencil sketches displayed next to the plants.

"These works are amazing!" remarked Poppy.

"They're all pretty special. I hope I'll get to work with brilliant artists like them in Cornwall." Nica's eyes twinkled.

Poppy squealed and clapped her hands over her mouth.

"Yes!" Nica jumped up and down.

"You got in! That's awesome. Oh my gosh, I can't believe you're going to be leaving."

"Neither can I. I can't wait."

"When do you go?"

"Would you believe next week?"

"Next week! But that's so soon. We won't even really have time to say goodbye."

"Bob and Rose want to hold a few drinks for me at the pub on Thursday, and you're the first person I've invited."

"I'll be there for sure."

"Be where?" a familiar voice chimed.

"Sis!" Poppy exclaimed with excitement as Rachael and Ben made their way around the tomato beds. "I'm so glad you're here."

Poppy threw her arms out as Ben ran toward her

with a big smile across his face. She planted a kiss on his little cheek and tickled him into a fit of laughter. "Aunty Pops," he giggled.

"So, tell me, what have I missed?"

"I'm moving to England for a bit to immerse myself in my art," glowed Nica as she gave Rachel a hug and introduced herself to Ben.

"O.M.G. Big news, congratulations," Rachel beamed, dropping her tote bag on the ground. Toppling out of it came snacks, a pair of tiny shorts, and a baby monitor.

Poppy shook her head. "No. Sis. Really? The baby monitor thing again. I thought you and Chris were doing well?"

"We are," Rachel laughed and wrapped her arms around Poppy, who planted a big kiss on her sister's cheek. "This isn't for us. This is for your fete. I thought we could use them as walkie-talkies. They work really well. Although," Rachel paused and rubbed her belly, "we will be needing them back soon," she added coyly.

"You're kidding? That's amazing news, congratulations!" Teary with joy, Poppy gave Rachel a hug, which Nica and Ben both joined.

"When are you due?" Nica asked.

"Six months!" Rachel squealed. "Turns out my reaction to Chris working so much was also fuelled by pregnancy hormones. I was shocked when I found out, but we're all over the moon and Chris has promised that after this weekend he's going to stop working so much."

"Well, you just make sure you enjoy yourself this weekend. No lifting for you," said Poppy seriously.

Rachel waved her hand lightly. "I'm pregnant, not ill," she said.

"Alright then. We better get to it. The masses will be here before we know it!"

Soon after Rachel arrived, Jen and Claris bustled in with baskets full of cupcakes. Tony followed closely with the Men's Shed gang. Everyone was buzzing. Nica focused on curating the layout of the exhibition, with the help of Ben and Rachel, who were making sure the labels for each artwork had been firmly attached to the easels. Ben thought it a very important job and Poppy loved the way his little face beamed with pride as each label was carefully secured into place. Tony and the other men started setting up the trestle tables and displaying their wood works for the stall.

By ten o'clock, Jen and Claris had tiers of cupcakes set up on rose patterned tablecloths. Vintage teapots filled with cut flowers adorned the tables and the urns bubbled away, ready to make cups of tea and coffee. Poppy got to work setting up the book sale stall, and Rose and Bob had the sausages sizzling by eleven. Poppy was surprised that people, no doubt enticed by the smell wafting down the road, had already started to arrive. Almost everyone remarked on how amazing the hub looked. And most of them were excited to find out what programs were on offer, except for Mr. Jenkins, of course, who rolled in on his scooter and complained that the children running around using the bubble blowers posed a safety hazard. He scooted off in a huff, adamant that such frivolity was unnecessary, and he was going to cancel his library membership. Poppy wasn't upset in the least.

In no time at all, the community garden was full of laughter and conversation. The cups of tea flowed, and the stalls were doing a roaring trade. Thomas and Aiden were pulling into the car park just as Nica came skipping over to where Poppy and Rachel stood helping customers at the bookstall. "The flyers really worked. Heaps of people have come up from Sydney."

Aiden emerged through the crowd carrying a box full of seedlings and a picnic basket. He smiled as he waved in their direction.

"Pops, your lover boy is here." Rachel winked.

"Wow, this *is* epic!" he said, steeling a kiss from Poppy's lips. His touch reminded her of last night and sent her spine tingling all over. "Look at all these people."

"I know, isn't it great? I never expected it would be this busy... Hi Thomas," Poppy called as Thomas smiled and walked over to inspect the tomatoes he'd planted last week.

"He's been talking about tomatoes and cut and come again lettuces all morning. I bought him a new phone so he could take photos of all the plants. He's better at using one than me—he's been taking videos and has asked me to set him up a YouTube account," mused Aiden.

"He's done such a great job. Truly, he's a star. This place wouldn't look as good as it does without all the work Thomas has put in."

"Yeah, he's pretty talented, my brother. He's been inspired by the chicken coop, almost finished," Aiden joked, "and now he wants to grow a new topiary in the shape of a rooster." Aiden put his hand up in mock resignation. Poppy loved how Aiden seemed to grace through life with gentleness. "So, where do you want me?" he asked excitedly.

Poppy giggled. Aiden's dimples and enthusiasm were infectious. "I want you naked in my bed," she whispered, "but until then, how about giving Bob and Rose a hand over at the sausage sizzle? They looked swamped."

The line for the sausage sizzle snaked through the

garden and onto the street. Poppy took a moment to soak up the atmosphere. Everyone was enjoying themselves and Ben and some of the other kids had started playing hide and go seek, using the baby monitors to talk to each other as they hid amongst the vegetable patches. Thomas was busy shooting little videos of seedlings and taking photos of the event.

Claris and Jen were frantically pulling more cupcakes out of the cooler boxes hidden under their table and topping up the bubbling urns. Little mounds of pink, cream, and dark chocolate iced cupcakes were soon covering the vintage rosette tablecloth. Stout floral teapots sat happily next to vases of lavender picked fresh from the herb garden. The feint aroma of earl grey wafted on a gentle breeze.

It didn't take long for the cupcakes to sell out and for the urns to empty. By the time the fete drew to a close and people started to meander off, Claris and Jen were exhausted and in need of something stronger than a cup of tea. They both suggested popping down to the pub for a celebratory drink.

"That sounds like a great idea," Poppy, recognising the voice instantly, turned to see none other than Charles Batsy swagger through the citrus. Manicured, as always, in a suit and freshly shined boots, he stood out, his ego palpable in the air around him. "WHISKY FOR EVERYONE," he called with his arms out wide.

"Charles, what are you doing here?" Poppy asked under her breath. "Have you been drinking?"

"I've been celebrating. Celebrating. I've only had, had a couple."

Poppy could see Aiden standing next to the Men's Shed watching her intently. She was conscious of his every move and although she didn't want to make a scene, she wished Charles would leave her alone. "I'm kinda busy, Charles."

"I can see. You've got yourself quite the community shindig here," he said in a way Poppy thought was slightly tainted by sarcasm. "I'm not sure why you're bothering though. You'll be back in the city before long. Can't wait to take you out to my local haunts. The boys will go crazy if I've got a pretty thing like you on my arm."

Poppy wasn't sure whether to accept Charles' words as a compliment or not. "Charles, I've got to go. But you should know I'm seeing..." Poppy didn't have a chance to finish. Before she knew it, Charles had pulled her against his body and planted his mouth over hers. He felt like a wet fish and smelt of bourbon. He held her so tightly she struggled to push him away. When he did finally stagger a step backwards, Poppy knew her skin was crimson read. It felt itchy and hot. But all she could think of was Aiden. She turned around shaking her head in his direction, hoping to God that he hadn't seen what had just happened. As her eyes met his, Poppy felt the blood drain from her cheeks. Her heart raced. Aiden stood, staring at her with a face full of pain and devastation. It was like someone had run a knife into his gut.

"Aiden, WAIT!" Yelled Poppy, pushing Charles out of the way. But it was too late. Aiden was already in his ute. His tyres screeched as he pulled out of the car park and sped off down the road, leaving Poppy in a dazed moment of shock.

Later that afternoon, Rachel and Nica sat in the library and listened to Poppy as she wailed. "I have no idea what happened today!" she cried.

"I mean, I had no idea Charles was going to come to the fete. I hadn't returned any of his texts or anything all week. I, I..." The tears started flowing again. "And now Aiden thinks I was going behind his back."

"I'm sure he doesn't think that, Poppy," Rachel consoled.

Nica nodded in agreement. "It's true. Aiden's a great guy. He's probably just a bit pissed off. It won't take him long to realise what's happened. Charles is an idiot and you've done nothing wrong."

Poppy sniffled. "I hope so. But he hasn't replied to any of my texts, and I've left at least three voice messages explaining that I had no idea Charles would be there. He hasn't replied to any of them. When he came to pick up Thomas, before we closed up, he didn't even look at me. It was like I wasn't even there, it's just that you're leaving, Nica and Rachel, you'll go back to the city with Ben," Poppy turned her gaze toward Ben who was engrossed in a book about farm animals. It always warmed her heart to see the library being enjoyed by little people. "And, well, I'll have no one. Maybe not even a job."

"Give him time," comforted Rachel. "You know what men are like? They get sulky and just need some space. And, if Carmel doesn't come back maybe they'll ask you to stay on."

"Maybe you're right." Poppy smiled weakly. "He'll be in the library tomorrow anyway. The final fire and safety maintenance inspection is booked. D-day. He did say, last week, that it was all good though."

"It will be fine," said Nica. Poppy was grateful for her and Rachel's support. She didn't know what she would do without their support. *Whatever happens tomorrow*, she thought, *at least I have them*—and Sven and Carl would be happy to have her back as their neighbour. But what Poppy wanted most of all, was to wake up every morning next to Aiden and eat fresh eggs for breakfast. She didn't want to move back to the city. And if she was honest with herself, she didn't really care whether or not her contract was renewed. The only thing she truly cared about right now was Aiden.

CHAPTER 20

At 9:00 am there was a loud knock on the door. Poppy trembled. It was Aiden come to carry out the final report.

"Hello." Poppy's voice shook with nerves.

Aiden still hadn't replied to any of her text messages, missed phone calls, or voice messages. She desperately wanted to explain how sorry she was for what had happened and that she had no idea Charles was going to kiss her. But Aiden had ghosted her, and it was breaking Poppy's heart. She didn't know what to do or say to make things better and now that he was in the library, she desperately wanted to make it right.

"Hi," he replied shortly.

Aiden looked uncomfortable in Poppy's presence. He diverted his eyes and avoided meeting her own. It was obvious he wanted to get today's inspection over as quickly as possible and that he had no intention of talking to her. He was stern and unforgiving and a completely different man than the one who'd made her breakfast and lit her fire just over forty-eight hours ago.

He walked around the library, silently. Poppy could have cut the air around him with a knife. He barely looked at her, let alone said anything. Instead, he continued to check off items on his clipboard. Poppy wanted to say something, but she didn't know what. Every time she went to open her mouth a customer caught her attention. If she had one more person ask if they could borrow a USB, she thought she might scream. Before she knew it, Aiden had inspected the other two buildings and was back in his ute. Her heart sank as he pulled out of the car park. Her moment had disappeared in a flash.

"What's the point Nica? Aiden has made it clear that he's not interested in talking. It's been two whole days since the fete." Poppy had ignored every message she'd received from Charles and had told him explicitly that she wasn't interested in dating. She slumped into the couch next to the fire. Not even a strong earl grey could solve this problem. Nica placed a tray carrying two teacups and a couple of shortbread biscuits onto the floor in front of them. Poppy could feel the tears well in her eyes and a lump form in her throat. The vision of the hurt on Aiden's face came flooding back to her. "He was pretty mad. It doesn't matter how many times I've tried to tell him I didn't want Charles to kiss me. He won't listen. He's made his mind up." Poppy sobbed. "Bloody Charles. Just when I'm finally happy. Just when I finally fall in love. Just..."

"Did you just say you've fallen in love?"

Poppy nodded silently.

"Poppy, here's what I know for sure," Nica said seriously. "Number one, my tarot cards definitely said that you were going to end up with your soul mate, and, number two, *'love never fails – it's the prize for which you run'*. And, if you love Aiden, you have to *tell* him, you have to talk to him. Give him a few days to come to his senses and see that you had no control over Charles' actions and then speak to him again."

"I just can't believe this is how it ends, Nica. We raise the money for this place, get it up to standard. Well, I think so. Aiden certainly gave nothing away this morning. Property Management and Assets will email me the report tomorrow. And then, that's it."

"That *isn't* it. I know it. Poppy, I've seen the way Aiden looks at you. Yeah he's pissed off but I'm sure he'll see reason," Nica said earnestly. "He's just angry. The guy is obviously crazy about you and the thought of you kissing anyone else has really upset him."

Poppy wiped the tears from her cheeks and nodded

again. "Okay," she sniffled. "I'll try talking to him again."

"It'll work out, Poppy. Just have some faith. Remember your lotus tattoo? Beauty blooms out of murky waters."

CHAPTER 21

The next morning Poppy arrived at the library early. After unlocking the doors and opening the windows, she sat at the front counter and braced herself as the monitor screen flashed on. She felt sick. The last two months had been all for this moment. She was proud of what they'd achieved in such a short space of time. The community hub had really come alive and Poppy could wholeheartedly say it was an important part of Derrin's local community. Her end of month report to the Council had detailed the achievements in library membership numbers, participants at the art studio, and Men's Shed, as well as the visitors to the garden. More people had enquired about volunteering and the gardens had received compliments from almost everyone who'd visited, so much so that Thomas had decided to start up his own small business helping people with their gardens around town.

Clicking the desktop icon for her inbox, Poppy took a slow steady deep breath before opening the email with the subject line *Fire and Safety Report*.

Dear Miss MacLuster,

We regret to inform you that the recent Fire and Safety Report came back negligent. Please refer to the attached document. Although we acknowledge the hard work you and your volunteers contributed in attempting to bring the buildings up to safety standards, they did not pass yesterday's inspection, and the Council has made the decision to decommission the library and community hub. Thus, your contract will not be renewed and will be terminated on the 30ᵗʰ of September at 5:00 pm. We wish to thank for you your service.

Kind regards,
Blair Switchel
Property Management and Assets
Derrin Shire Council.

Poppy's hands shook. She felt lightheaded, as if the blood had been drained from her body. She couldn't believe what she was reading. They didn't pass the inspection. Why hadn't Aiden told her she hadn't got it right? Why did he say things were fine when they obviously were not? Was he just trying to get back at her for something she had no control over? Poppy fumed. She was seconds away form bursting into tears.

Just then Aiden walked up the library's entrance steps. His face seemed softer than when she'd last seen him. His eyes looked watery with emotion. *How dare he think he can come here after this?* Poppy couldn't believe that Aiden would stoop so low. Fair enough, he was angry with her, but he didn't have to ruin it for everyone else. Especially when they'd worked so hard to fix up the library and community hub grounds. Trembling, she gripped the copies of the inspection report and email from Council, as they released from the staff printer.

"Hello," Aiden smiled, softly as he pushed the library door open.

She didn't reply. Instead, she stared straight through him and wished her eyes were daggers.

"Look, Poppy, I've come to apologise for overreacting about Charles." There was shyness about Aiden that Poppy was now only too happy to ignore. "He's a jerk and I'm sorry I didn't believe you." Aiden chewed the corner of his bottom lip. "I'm an idiot. I just... it's just... I didn't know what to do. And when I saw you there, Saturday, in his arms, I..."

"So being angry about Charles was reason enough to ruin things here, was it? You might not care about me,

Aiden, but what about Thomas and Clive and Steve and, and..." Tears streamed down Poppy's cheeks. She hated showing Aiden that he had hurt her so much when he stood there not even attempting to look sorry about the safety report. "You know what? Just forget it." Poppy cried and shook her head. That Aiden had stooped so low hurt her terribly. Not giving him a chance to explain, she pushed past him and ran into the library backroom, locking the door behind her.

"POPPY,' he called after her. "Poppy, I *do* care about you. I don't know what you're talking about."

Poppy sank to the floor and sobbed. Her eyes felt swollen. She held an icepack against her face, hoping to look respectable for opening the library doors at 9:00 am. There was no way she could stay in Derrin now. There would be no library. No cottage. No Nica. And definitely no Aiden. Poppy couldn't believe that after everyone's hard work, it was Aiden's signature that ended it all. Yet, there it was, plain as day, on the report. And there was nothing she could do about it.

Poppy sat on the lounge room floor, saying goodbye to Page Cottage. Her guts swirled. She was devastated to have to leave her new home and friends. But how could she stay when the man she loved had so obviously rejected her? It had been easy for her to negotiate to end her contract early. Council's Human Resources had okayed her application within hours, making Poppy feel like if it was that simple, to end her employment, she must be making the right decision. She hadn't gone to Nica's goodbye drinks. She couldn't face seeing everyone in her heartbroken state. She'd so believed that the community hub was saved and felt that she'd let everyone down. And Aiden hadn't so much as said 'boo' this last week. He'd all but disappeared and Poppy couldn't help but wish that he had made a bit of an effort to acknowledge that he'd let her down. But the last two days he'd turned into a ghost. His ute hadn't even been in the driveway and Poppy wondered if he'd left town. She wasn't sure what to do.

Sniffling, she wiped her nose with a tissue and blotted her eyes. The last thing she wanted to do was pack her bags and leave, but she had no choice. She couldn't stay. Not when the man she loved had betrayed her so badly. Poppy would have stayed crying on the floor all afternoon, but a knock on the door forced her to her feet. It was Nica.

"*Poppy,*" Nica beamed.

"Is this about your residency?" Poppy asked, wiping her eyes.

Nica shook her head. She bit her bottom lip. She, too, looked like she was about to burst into tears.

"What? What's up?" Poppy thought it must be

serious. Shaking with excitement, Nica held a mobile in her hand. It looked familiar.

"Aiden didn't sign the report."

"What do you mean? His signature is right here." Poppy pulled the copy of the report she'd printed from her email, out of her handbag.

Nica shook her head. "No, he didn't. Charles, the bastard, got Mattie Boyle to rewrite the report and use Aiden's signature. Do you remember you told me that Charles had been caught up at the rodeo in a business meeting with Mattie and that Mattie had come into his inheritance and was buying all these rounds?" Poppy nodded as Nica continued. "They fudged it and lodged it with Charles' dad, Derek Batsy the MP, who somehow got it through Council. Aiden's report never even reached the Property Assets and whatever they call themselves." Poppy couldn't believe what she was hearing. If this was true, the community hub could still be saved.

"How do you know all this?" she asked.

"You know those baby monitors?"

Poppy nodded.

"Well, Thomas was shooting video on his new phone of the herbs he'd planted near the art studio. He'd found one of the baby monitors near the scarecrow and had put it in his pocket. Ben, or one of his friends, must have dropped the other baby monitor near the back of the art studio where Charles had parked his Land Rover.

They were both still on and Thomas' video picked up a conversation Charles was having with Mattie just after he kissed you. Here listen..."

Poppy's mouth fell open. She couldn't believe what she was hearing. *"Ah, Mattie, mate, it's in the bag now. She's definitely keen on me. I knew getting her all lusted up would make it easier."*

"Hell, Yeah! Aiden's bloody pissed too. He's a damn sook, if you ask me—has been since high school," another voice commented. Poppy assumed it was Mattie's.

"She'll never suspect that I'm a signature away from buying the land off of Council, once everything falls into place—all those bloody meetings. Dad has been working toward it for months, diverting the funding elsewhere. And good-old mum has been making sure the place looked as run down as possible. After Carmel took stress leave, Mum even deleted members from the system who hadn't borrowed in over a month just to make the place look more unused and more of a liability. It almost bloody worked, too. I totally didn't expect Poppy to love it so much here, though, being a city girl and all. Oh, man! I felt pretty uneasy when I saw how much money they'd bloody raised and the number of people that had started using this dump again. But with you being able to jimmy the report to make it look like Aiden didn't pass it on inspection—

we'll be building units on this land before you know it—
your investment has been a wise one, mate."

"Sure has. The first unit development in Derrin. The
return on investment will be massive. Get me out of this
bloody fireman's uniform, I say."

"I'm hoping Poppy won't find out though, because
I've kinda grown to like her. She's effing sexy in a
library way, mate. You know what I mean?"

Nica put Thomas's mobile down. "He'll want it back
soon," she said, nodding her head toward the next door.

Poppy was lost for words. What she just heard
changed everything. "Nica, this is big. This explains
why Gladys was so aloof when I asked about the
budget. It explains why all the newish books had been
deleted. Why the WiFi router was shoved in the
cupboard. Why the self-serve was never installed. Why
memberships dropped off rapidly and why the place was
in a shambles. Gladys was working for her son this
whole time." Poppy started to panic. "What do we do
now?"

Nica, a sea of calm, spoke as though she had things
sorted. "Tony has taken a recording of the message and
he and the other volunteers are at the Council chambers
as we speak. Neither Charles nor Mattie have been
seen."

"And what about Aiden?" Poppy felt sick that she'd
accused Aiden of being so underhanded. He'd been

innocent all along. How was he ever going to forgive her?

Nica fell silent. "I haven't seen him. Thomas is next door and a friend of theirs is staying with him. I'm not sure how to get hold of him either. I'm sorry."

Poppy's heart sank.

CHAPTER 22

Poppy sat on the front steps of Page Cottage waiting for Nica to pick her up. Sunlight poured over her. Everything smelt fresh and invigorated by the morning's reprieve from the cold. She was due to get on the next train. In thirty minutes, she'd be on her way back to the city and the couch she'd reserved at Rachel's place until her flat was available again. She thought it ironic that today—when her heart felt so cold—was the warmest day she'd experienced in Derrin, so far.

Aiden was no-where to be seen. It had been two days since she'd found out Charles and Mattie manipulated the report. Poppy hadn't been able to contact Aiden, and she'd left countless voicemail messages. The friend looking after Thomas had mentioned something about Aiden being back in a couple of days but not sure when.

Poppy was grateful for Nica's offer to drive her to the station, especially since Nica had her own packing to do. Poppy was going to miss her new best friend. She couldn't believe how much she'd fallen in love with Page Cottage, Derrin and the country life. Even Mr. Jenkins would be missed—just. She had wanted to say goodbye to Thomas, but he was out. The thought of not being able to give him or Aiden at least a thank you hug broke Poppy's heart.

The only one she had said farewell to was Mr. Meow, who had briefly appeared from under the mulberry tree carrying a mouse, only to be scared off by Nica's Bumblebee.

"See ya, buddy," Poppy whispered as his black body darted under the house.

Nica waved as she got out of the car and popped the boot. "Any word?" she asked softly.

Poppy couldn't bring herself to speak. Instead, she shook her head and swallowed hard. "Let's just go," she said eventually. Placing the keys in the letterbox, she turned to Page Cottage and breathed deeply, taking a moment to soak in its detail. Poppy never wanted to forget its charm. She couldn't believe she would never set eyes on its run-down weatherboards or leadlight window ever again. "I'll never forget you," she muttered with one last goodbye.

The drive to the train station felt a lifetime. Poppy found it hard to watch the open green paddocks pass by. She had only been in Derrin for just under three months and had been so busy she hadn't really stopped to feel the Kikuyu under her feet. As they drove into town and turned into Cock Ball Street, Poppy could feel a lump form in her throat and her heart pounding.

"Are you sure you don't want to try him one more time?" Nica asked as she pulled on the handbrake.

"It's no use. He doesn't want to talk to me," Poppy whispered as Nica's hand wrapped around her own. It was warm and comforting. "I'm going to miss you," she said.

"I'll miss you too," replied Nica, wiping a tear from her cheek.

Poppy walked around to the boot and lifted her suitcase onto the road. Lost in her own sadness, she didn't hear the voice that called to her from across the road.

"Wait! POPPY," the familiar voice called again.

Poppy's heart skipped a beat. She could feel the blood pump through her veins. Jogging across the road, in jeans and the same flannelette shirt he'd been wearing the night they first crossed paths, was Aiden.

"Wait!" he called as he ran toward her.

"Aiden?"

"Poppy, I'm so sorry," he said as his body landed next to hers. "Don't go."

"Aiden, where have you been? I've been trying to get hold of you. I thought you didn't want anything to do with me. You didn't answer any of my calls or texts." Poppy cried.

Aiden's brown eyes filled with tears. "Poppy, I'm so sorry. I heard what Charles and Mattie did, and I went straight to my solicitor's office in Sydney. I wanted to be able to come to you and tell you I could save the library and community hub. It took longer than I thought, and my phone battery died. I'm so sorry."

"But I went next door to see Thomas and your friend didn't mention anything about any of this. And I went by again this morning, but no one was home."

"They didn't know. I left quickly. I didn't have time to explain. Thomas has gone out to buy chickens. He wanted to surprise you with fresh eggs when he next saw you. I only just got back. I went to Page Cottage to find you, but everything was locked up..." Aiden's voice choked. "I thought I'd missed you." Aiden looked into Poppy's eyes. Gently, he lifted the wayward strands of hair that brushed against her forehead and tenderly tucked them behind her ear.

"Aiden, I'm so sorry I accused you of deliberately writing a negative report. I should have believed you when you said you didn't know anything about it."

Aiden shook his head and took Poppy's face into his hands. His fingers wiped away the tears that flowed down her cheeks. "You weren't to know. And I was a jerk. Poppy, please don't go. Stay."

"But I have nowhere to live and no job."

"Well, I can't promise my solicitor will be able to save the library and community hub, but he thinks he has enough evidence to be able to cancel any contract that may have already been signed for the sale of the land. Plus, Council wouldn't have acted if they had of know the whole thing was a sham. And you've got community backing and that's what counts."

"Even so, I have nowhere to go."

"Yes, you do," Aiden said softly. "I love you, Poppy. Come home with me."

Poppy felt the tears well in her eyes. Aiden's thumb rubbed against her lotus tattoo. "I love you too," she smiled. Without another word, Poppy reached up and wrapped her arms around Aiden's neck. Her heartbeat fiercely as she felt the warmth of his lips against her own.

"YAY." Nica, who had stood by quietly this whole time, could no longer contain her excitement and whooped in the air. "I knew my tarot cards were right!"

Poppy couldn't help but giggle. "I don't know about tarot cards," she said, brushing Aiden's cheek with her fingertips and smiling warmly, "but you do feel like home."

EPILOGUE

Poppy shivered against one of the old weatherboard station houses that edged the tracks at Derrin Station. The bottom of her polka dot skirt was drenched. *Lucky I wore my gumboots—this weather is blimmin British.* It had been almost a year since Poppy had seen her best friend, and not even the torrential rain and icy winds could dampen her excitement. Any moment now, Nica's train would pull into the station.

Poppy had been on the count down since early that morning. She'd woken just as the sunlight peeked into hers and Aiden's bedroom. Not even Thomas and Mr. Meow had been awake, and they were usually up before everyone—Thomas eager to get to his job, as Head Gardener, at the community hub and Mr. Meow eager for food.

Poppy snuggled into Aiden as he came to stand

beside her. She wrapped her cold hands into his flannelette jacket and pressed her cheek against his chest for warmth.

"How many minutes 'til arrival?" he asked, his teeth chattering.

"Any moment now... eek, there it is," chirped Poppy. She pointed down the tracks. Piercing the rain and mist were two large headlights. "I can't wait to see her."

Aiden chuckled. "Not long now, honey. You guys have a lot to catch up on. But, remind me, why is Nica home early?"

Poppy shrugged her shoulders. "She didn't say. All I know is she's on that train. And I'm so glad she's back. The community hub isn't the same without her. She was over the moon when I told her the Council had revoked their decision to close the library and sell its land. Your solicitors were amazing finding all that evidence against Charles and Mattie—talk about fraud. And the petition that you and Thomas got together definitely made all the difference, I still can't believe over two thousand people signed it. Derrin doesn't even have that many people living in it."

"Let's just say a lot of tourists were appalled to hear that the only free Wi-Fi spot in town was about to disappear. Plus, after the fete, heaps of people realised how important the community hub is and so did the councillors."

"Well, whatever the reason people signed, I'm truly

grateful. I really didn't think I was going to get to keep my job."

"And now that they've made you permanent, there's no stopping you." Aiden leant down and brushed his lips against Poppy's. The touch of his mouth to hers warmed her whole body. For a moment, she forgot about why they were standing in the freezing cold. That was until a familiar voice chimed across the platform.

"Will you two get a room?" it called.

Poppy pulled herself from Aiden's embrace. There, like a beacon of sunshine, was Nica, dressed in bright yellow jeans and a sunflower clad raincoat, with a rainbow-striped suitcase in tow. Poppy ran toward her, with arms out wide. "It's really you," she squealed.

"It's really me," laughed Nica as she held Poppy close. "We shouldn't stay out here too long though, you're getting drenched."

"You brought the weather back with you," Poppy giggled. "Come on, the fireplace is roaring back at the cottage. I've got proper black tea and freshly baked ginger-nut biscuits ready, and I want to hear *everything.*"

Poppy handed Nica a hot mug of tea strong enough to wake the dead.

"This cup of tea may just be my favourite one yet,"

Nica smiled. She closed her eyes in satisfaction as she sipped the brew. "I've missed hanging out with you. It's nice of Aiden to leave us alone to talk for a bit. I really needed our chats a couple of months ago."

Poppy frowned and passed her friend another ginger-bread biscuit, she'd been snacking on them ever since they'd perched themselves on the stools at the kitchen bench and Poppy wondered if she should have made a second batch. "What's wrong? Why did you come back early?"

"Oh, you know. The usual. Nica meets a guy, guy turns out to be a jerk. It's not the reason I'm back, though." Nica paused and took another sip of tea. "I just felt it was time," she added simply. "My exhibition was over, and I felt homesick. Which surprised me because I really thought I'd be backpacking through Europe next summer, but one morning I woke up with this urgency to come home." Nica snapped the biscuit in two. "So, I did."

"Well, I'm glad to have you back. It hasn't been the same around here without you. We've really missed you at the hub. And Thomas hasn't stopped talking about you since you called to say you were getting on a plane. He'll be home soon. He's gardening today."

"I can't wait to see him, either. It's so awesome that you still have your job and the library is saved. I mean, what a tosser that Charles was."

"I know, right? No one has seen him, or Mattie,

since. Gladys and Derek Batsy have conveniently gone on a cruise to Europe. I doubt they'll be back anytime soon. Will you try to come back to the art centre now that you're home?" Poppy waited as Nica scrunched her damp hair. Her red ringlets bounced happily.

"I don't think so. I'm not sure what I'll do yet. I think I'm just going to take a breather for a bit and wait to see what opportunities come knocking. I can't thank you enough for letting me stay in Page Cottage."

"Well, I pretty much live here, with Aiden, but the cottage is still mine to have for as long as I work at the library. I sometimes go over there to meditate, and Aiden and I sometimes use it when we need some alone time—if you know what I mean," Poppy winked. "But really, it's just sitting there. You're welcome to stay there for as long as you need. Aiden even stacked the fireplace for you."

"So, things are going great for you guys?"

Poppy took a long sip of her tea and leant against the bench. "Better than great," she grinned. Reaching into her pocket, she pulled out a little blue box and carefully opened the lid. There, inside, was a stunning solitaire diamond set on top of an elegant platinum band.

Nica squeaked.

"Aiden asked me to marry him." Poppy still couldn't believe she was saying those words. "He asked me the other night in front of the fire. Thomas was having a sleepover at a mate's place. It was just the two of us and we'd finished a takeaway curry when he presented some Champagne. The ring was at the bottom of my glass. We needed to get it resized and picked it up from the jeweller before we met you." Poppy's heart opened as she slipped the sparkling engagement ring onto her finger.

"It's beautiful," gushed Nica. "Congratulations, I'm so happy for you guys. Maybe that's why I had to come home, to help you with your wedding planning. Although, I'm sure Rachel is stoked."

"She screamed down the phone when I told her." Poppy had been in fits of laughter at her sister's reaction. It was the most hysterical she'd ever heard Rachel be. "She'll be here this weekend with Ben and little Rosie. Rosie's the cutest baby ever. Now, we just need to find *you* a man."

Nica snorted. "Nah, I'm having a self imposed period of celibacy. I've got to figure out a few things first, primarily where I'm going to live. I can't stay in Page Cottage forever."

Poppy breathed deeply and looked out the kitchen window toward the backyard. There was Aiden, taking advantage of a break in the weather and putting away Thomas' chickens, his muscles firm under his damp shirt. Poppy smiled with amusement and remembered the day she had stood in front of him, unaware that her nipples were on show. It felt like a lifetime ago.

"Sometimes," she mused, putting down her cup of

tea and rubbing her lotus tattoo with her thumb, "the Universe has a great sense of humour. We might not always know how our dreams will come true but, with a little faith, we always know they will come true. Home is nearly always much closer than you think," she smiled. "And there's no other place like it."

IN GRATITUDE

To my friends and family, thank you so very much for believing in my creative spirit. Thank you to Mum and Dad for supporting my creative endeavours, no matter how big, whacky or heavy. Thank you to my sister for always having a laugh and listening to my stories. Thank you to my Love, for believing in me and supporting me through those long nights I was up tapping away on my keyboard. Thank you to my daughter—your divine presence is inspiring me to 'go for it' and words will never do justice to how much I love you. Thank you to my Nana for always asking 'how's the book going?' and to my Nan who's always up for a chat about what she's reading. Thank you to my most wonderful friend, Amy, who has been there for me since high school. Thank you to my friend and publisher, Sarah, for believing that my words were worthy enough to be shared. And a big shout out and thanks to all the public librarians who give tirelessly to their community on the daily—you all rock!

And lastly, thank you to the creative Spirit that runs through all of us and calls us to create. Without your never-ending presence I would not have dared to dream large enough to put pen to paper or brush to canvas—thank you. xo

ABOUT THE AUTHOR

Amiee MacRae lives in the rolling countryside, of Southeast Queensland, with her firefighting fiancé, wee daughter, energetic pooch, rather large cat, four wonky rescue chickens and adopted porch rooster. After many years working in galleries, and a short stint teaching very small humans, Aimee became a public librarian with a soft spot for quirky characters. When she's not crafting her next novel, you can find her behind an art easel or knee deep in garden compost. Either way, she'll be accompanied by a strong cup of earl grey and copious amounts of shortbread.

MORE FROM SERENADE PUBLISHING

Brigadier Station Series

By Sarah Williams:

The Brothers of Brigadier Station

The Sky over Brigadier Station

The Legacies of Brigadier Station

Christmas at Brigadier Station (An Outback Christmas Novella)

The Outback Governess (A Sweet Outback Novella)

Heart of the Hinterland Series

By Sarah Williams:

The Dairy Farmer's Daughter

Their Perfect Blend

Beyond the Barre

A Dying Second Sun

by Peter A. Dowse

Winner Winner Chicken Dinner

by Sarah Jackson

A New Page

by Aimee MacRae

Middle Women

By Jack Garrety

Mim and Wiggy's Grand Adventure

By Jay McKenzie

For more information visit:

www.serenadepublishing.com

The Dairy Farmer's Daughter

(#1 in the Heart of the Hinterland series)

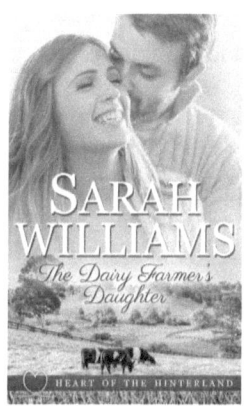

Will Justin choose riches over his heritage or will he find a love more valuable than all the money in the world?

Justin would have preferred to stay in the city and pretend it was an ordinary day. A day that didn't include a funeral for a father he'd barely known...

Justin Wheeler is not a country boy. He could have been, if his mother had stayed married to his father and not moved back to the city when he was only a toddler. But now that his estranged father is dead and he has inherited the dairy farm, Justin finds himself considering if the life he is living is actually the life he wants.

Family means everything to Freya Montgomery. She loves

living on the land and helping to grow the family business. She knows how important agriculture is to their small hinterland community, so when Justin arrives in town and is offered a generous price from a housing developer to buy his property, Freya must convince him not to accept the deal and instead lease the land to her family.

The Dairy Farmer's Daughter is the first novella in an exciting new sexy, small-town series called "Heart of the Hinterland" by Bestselling author, Sarah Williams.

Buy The Dairy Farmer's Daughter

The Brothers of Brigadier Station

(#1 in the Brigadier Station series)

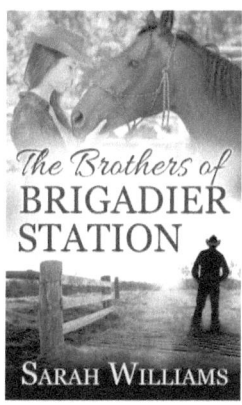

She came to the outback to marry the love of her life. She just didn't expect him to be her fiancé's younger brother.

When Meghan Flanagan, a vet-nurse from Townsville, moves to Brigadier Station in outback Queensland to marry the man of her dreams, she is shocked to discover that perhaps her fiancé isn't the man she wants waiting for her at the altar. The man she's destined to marry, just might be his younger brother.

Cautious of women after a disastrous past relationship, Darcy is happy living on his beloved cattle station, spending his spare time riding horses, going to rodeos and campdrafting. He didn't expect the perfect woman show up on his doorstep. Engaged to his brother.

With the wedding only hours away, Meghan must make the

decision of a lifetime. But, her betrayal could tear the family apart. She knows all too well the pain of losing loved ones and being alone.

Now that she has the family she so desperately wants; will she risk losing it all?

Buy The Brothers of Brigadier Station

The Sky over Brigadier Station

(#2 in the Brigadier Station series)

He guards his heart. She yields to no man. Will a chance encounter set a course for true love?

Noah McGuire buries his demons deep inside. But when he's forced to return home to Brigadier Station to collect his inheritance, he can no longer avoid digging up his painful past. With the wounds of childhood trauma reopened, his world plunges into darkness until a beautiful pilot sets his heart afire.

Riley Sinclair isn't afraid to fly against the wind. While the spunky helicopter pilot's cattle herding business ruffles the feathers of most men, the handsome Noah seems different. But as demand for her skills grows, she worries that giving into passion could keep her dreams grounded.

As their chemistry soars, an unexpected tragedy throws their lives and their budding romance into a tailspin.

Can Noah and Riley leave their baggage behind to let love fly free?

The Sky over Brigadier Station is the second standalone book in the captivating Brigadier Station Western romance series. If you like flawed characters, simmering scenes, and stunning Australian and New Zealand settings, then you'll love Sarah Williams' rugged tale.

Buy The Sky over Brigadier Station

The Legacies of Brigadier Station

(#3 in the Brigadier Station series)

Can Lachie be the father Hannah needs? And the man Abbie deserves?

Lachie McGuire is trying to make a fresh start. He's sobered up and is making amends for all the people he has hurt and the pain he has caused. But some of his past actions have consequences. Even if he doesn't remember them.

Needing her independence, single-mum Abbie Forsyth accepted a nursing position in the small outback town of Julia Creek and uprooted her daughter, Hannah from the only life she had ever known. Now, in the dusty, sun burned land they are creating a life together, just the two of them.

When Lachie is injured and needs medical assistance, Abbie is there for him. She's by his side every step of the way, including letting him stay with them while he recovers from surgery. But Abbie knows how volatile life with an addict can be and she has to think about her daughter's safety above her own growing affection for the handsome grazier.

Then tragedy strikes the small rural town and secrets begin to unravel...

Return to the Outback for the third instalment in the bestselling Brigadier Station series.

Buy The Legacies of Brigadier Station